INCIDENT AT COYOTE WELLS

John Magadan escapes the hang-man's noose, but his ride through the Sonora Desert bristles with violence and danger: he's pursued by Sheriff Tom Driscoll's posse; the Corson gang want the treasure which they feel they have been cheated out of; the Yaqui Indians want his horse and his blood. Beth Tolliver knows that Magadan holds the key to free her brother from Yuma prison — and something else . . . and she's decided that Magadan will stay to the bitter, bloody end.

Books by Logan Winters
in the Linford Western Library:

OVERLAND STAGE

LOGAN WINTERS

INCIDENT AT COYOTE WELLS

Complete and Unabridged

LINFORD
Leicester

First published in Great Britain in 2007 by
Robert Hale Limited
London

First Linford Edition
published 2008
by arrangement with
Robert Hale Limited
London

British Library CIP Data

Winters, Logan
    Incident at Coyote Wells.—Large print ed.—
Linford western library
1. Western stories
2. Large type books
I. Title
823.9′2 [F]

ISBN 978–1–84782–245–1

Published by
F. A. Thorpe (Publishing)
Anstey, Leicestershire

Set by Words & Graphics Ltd.
Anstey, Leicestershire
Printed and bound in Great Britain by
T. J. International Ltd., Padstow, Cornwall

1

My buckskin horse stood trembling beneath the torrid Arizona sky. His legs were unsteady, his flanks streaked with salt flecks. His head hung miserably as he pawed weakly at the sun-dried earth where water should have been. There were only dish-sized, curling plates of colorless mud there, baked into a sort of primitive mosaic. Brown cattails clustered around the dry waterhole, their heavy heads hanging like stunned mourners.

A white sky hung over the lifeless white land as I dragged myself up the side of a sand dune to search the terrain beyond, thinking that maybe there was some water to be had, that Coyote Wells still held some promise of life.

Peering into the distances from the top of the dune I saw nothing but more barren, formless land where nothing lived and nothing moved. I made my way to the scant shade of a group of thorny mesquite bushes and sagged down to the earth. Bees searched the mesquite flowers and a cluster of gnats drifted annoyingly around my head. I didn't bother to wave them away even when they tormented my ears and tried to swarm around my nostrils. I sat cross-legged, staring across the long sterile distances, my lips blistered, my tongue swollen with thirst.

Well, then, that was that — I was never going to make California now. I had come down from the piney hills around Flagstaff on to the shimmering desert where the devil winds blew and ghostly blue mirages danced, deceitfully promising coolness. A lot of men had died out on this desert and it looked like I was going to meet some of them soon. The old-timers I had asked had assured me that there was water at Coyote Wells if I could make it that far, always was. I could see that there had been — once. And I could see the bones of a desert sheep lying at the edge of the dry pool. It, too, had believed that the dry lake could sustain life.

I rolled on to my back, the lacework of shade from the narrow mesquite bushes criss-crossing my body. I threw my forearm over my eyes and tried to rest for just a little while. I could make it, I convinced myself. Even if the buckskin could not go on, I could make it. After dark, maybe. If I did not lose my way in the vastness.

I was dry, not a drop of perspiration to cool me. The gusting, sand-laden, arid wind dried and whipped away any moisture before it had time to form. It parched my mouth. Tightened my throat, dried my flesh. I should never have left Flagstaff, never. But then there had been no choice with that murder charge hanging over my head . . .

It was an hour or so on that the Indians came.

I must have heard them talking. Something caused my swollen eyelids to flicker open, to reach for my sun-heated rifle and roll over on to my belly. Instinct. I even imagined for a moment that Driscoll had somehow raised a posse to follow me on to this godforsaken desert.

There were two Indians only, that I could see. Yaquis. Short, dark men of the desert. One of them carried an old Army-issue .45–70 Springfield rifle. The other, apparently a younger warrior, had only a bow and a quiver of arrows. It was obvious that they were heading directly toward me, toward Coyote Wells, hoping for relief themselves. Suddenly they exchanged a few excited words. The younger Indian pointed eagerly. They had spotted my buckskin horse. I gritted my teeth and worked my body lower into the sand at the rise of the dune. They must have been thinking that this was their lucky day. I could have told them that it wasn't.

I removed my hat and watched as they approached the dry pond. I couldn't hear, and would not have understood their words, but I could sense their joy fading to dismay. There was no water. The horse was weak, tottering, almost useless. They nevertheless went to the buckskin, hoping I assumed, to try to get a few miles out of him to save their burning feet.

I fired one shot, not trying to kill. Sand kicked up at their feet and the older man who had taken the buckskin's reins dropped them, peering up at me through the brilliant glare of the white-hot day. He didn't like what he saw.

His .45–70 fired one shot at a time, needing to be reloaded after each. I made sure he saw the muzzle of my needle gun, a sixteen-shot Winchester repeater. He wanted no part of it, and besides I had the high ground. There was no discussion between the two Yaquis, no challenge. They simply turned and trudged out again on to the open desert in pursuit of water. Perhaps they knew of hidden springs no white man had ever discovered. I found myself wishing them luck.

Their appearance, however, nudged me into motion, reminding me that in the desert water is life and all creatures — man or beast will seek it out. Coyote Wells was a well-known source, although it was now dry. I hadn't known that; the Yaquis hadn't even known that it was dry. Therefore it was a magnet for all and sundry wandering the bleak wilderness. Even — although I still considered the possibility remote — for Sheriff Tom Driscoll. I raised myself to my feet and staggered down the sandy slope to collect the buckskin's reins.

I didn't mount the struggling beast, but led him along, hoping somehow to find water that would yet allow the suffering horse to recover from the ill-use I had given it. I watched over my shoulder as I trudged though the heavy white sand, knowing that Indians are notional and the Yaquis might yet decide to come back. Too, they might have had friends around that I had not seen. I wanted to put as much distance between myself and Coyote Wells as possible.

I glanced at the white sun, falling in its slow arc toward the eastern horizon. Two hours, I judged and the land would cool. And by midnight with no clouds to contain the heat of the day, the temperature would drop with astonishing speed to near-freezing, the night bringing no relief, but only a different sort of torment.

I saw the discarded blanket beside the trail before I had noticed the hoofprints. Three sets of them. There was a feeble keening in the air, nearly the sound of wind, but there was no breeze stirring across the white desert at that moment. Frowning, I paused, unsheathed my Winchester and peered into the harsh sunlight.

I saw — thought I saw — a human hand lift from the silver-hot sand and backed away instinctively. The sound rose again, like something calling from its grave, and I moved toward it with cautious apprehension. Then I heard the strangled, dry words clear enough to identify them.

'Help me. For God's sake!'

I knew he was a living man because he had called me. Had I not, I could have mistaken the huddled, drift-sand covered figure lying in a depression of the sun-bright dune as a dead animal or a sorry clump of brush.

He called me again, eagerly. I could go no faster than I was already traveling. I waded across the sand dune, dropping the reins to the fatigued buckskin along my way and went to my knees beside this sorry man. The sun glared down, hot on my back. My body shaded his eyes, pale, red, encrusted.

'Thank God!' he said in a whisper. 'Water, please! For God's sake.'

I could only shake my head and he understood. His throat was too dry for him to swallow as he tried to form a few words with badly split lips.

'They gunned me down. I thought I

could make Coyote Wells, find water . . . but they jumped me. We fought for a minute, then they just gunned me down like a dog.'

I couldn't answer. What was there to say, anyway?

'What's your name, friend?' he asked out of the parched canyon of his throat.

'Magadan.'

'Magadan, you've got to tell her what happened. She'll be waiting for me in Yuma . . . do that one thing for me.'

'Sure,' I promised. I was aware that I was lying to a dead man, but maybe it would ease his passing. Even had I wanted to go to Yuma, I would never be able to make it, the state I was in. I wasn't much more alive than this lost soul.

'I don't know who they were.' He sat up abruptly, astonishing me, grabbing the collar of my shirt with surprising strength. 'It had to have been Corson, though.' He fell back against the sand. After a few minutes of convulsed, ragged breathing, he uncupped his right hand and showed me what it held. An embossed German-silver button from a fancy vest or jacket.

'Take this, Magadan. I tore it off him during the fight. It'll be evidence. She'll know what to do.'

His breathing grew more sporadic, his eyes remained closed. I took the silver button and tucked it into the pocket of my jeans. Why, I don't know. I had no intention of going to Yuma. I was on the run myself, and making heavy going of it.

He breathed out his last words painfully. 'Just tell Beth that Ray did his best for her.'

And then he died.

I sat there, hunkered on my heels for a long time. I eased my conscience about lying to the dead man by running through what he had told me and realizing that even were I willing and able, he had designed an impossible task. Go to Yuma, find a woman named Beth, tell her that someone named Ray was dead and a man named Corson

10

was responsible. And then? Then nothing.

I had done all I could do. Listened to him, eased his mind. I searched his clothes, found a black leather wallet which I pocketed and little else. No matter — I would be lucky to make it to sundown myself. I couldn't have cared about any valuables he might be carrying. Nothing was of more value just then than water, and it couldn't be purchased at any price.

I'm ashamed to say I didn't take the time to bury the man. I didn't have the strength, which also embarrassed me. John Magadan — me — always worked his way with the strength of his two hands and broad shoulders, be it droving, lumberjacking, mining or harvesting. True, those three months in the Flagstaff jail had leaned me down some, but I had still had enough strength to overpower deputy Larson and break out when he let his guard down. Now I was nothing but a scarecrow, my body deprived of water and nourishment, wandering desperately toward an uncertain goal in California.

The blast furnace winds began again and sand started drifting across us — me and the gaunted, trail-beaten buckskin horse. It stung my eyes, obscured vision. I wondered what aspect we presented. A gaunt man leading a gaunt horse stumbling across an endless white desert.

With the dusk the wind subsided. I sagged to the ground, holding the shuddering buckskin's reins. The western skies had begun to darken. A long crimson pennant was streaked against the purpling sky and the waves of dunes began to turn blue and cast confused shadows against one another.

I doubted that I could go on.

I must have slept, because when I next opened my eyes a white half-moon was silvering the sands and the buckskin was nudging me, still expecting some human help for its misery. I had to grip the horse's bridle to boost myself to my feet again.

I stood surveying the moonscape of the desert. Nothing moved, there was no sound, no habitation, no animals abroad. Only endless night, endless sand.

I had to move with the coolness of night. Reluctantly I offered a silent apology to the buckskin horse and swung into the saddle. We continued on our way southward, trudging through the misery of the night. The horse's head hung. I clung to the pommel, fearful of falling from the weary saddle. The moon sailed higher, mocking our small attempts.

Sometimes after midnight I sensed that something had changed. I could hear the buckskin's hoofs clicking against solid earth, not whooshing through deep sand. Heavily I lifted my head and looked around me. I saw a thicket of nopal, a shaggy Joshua tree and here and there saguaro cactus rising tall and somehow menacing from the earth, their uplifted arms casting long shadows.

The land had begun to rise and break into arroyos and rocky hills. Distantly I saw a low range of sawtooth mountains. It was no relief. We were no nearer to fording water than we had been on the white desert.

In the far distance I saw a brief sparkle of light, no brighter than a firefly. I rubbed my eyes with an uncertain hand. The light was gone when I looked again. Had I actually seen a light or glimpsed a low desert star through a notch in the hills? I could not be certain, but it was a glimmer of hope and continuing as we were could only lead to death when the morning sun returned with its searing haunt.

I turned the buckskin's head toward the tiny beacon of promise.

Discovering the head of a dry wash which angled down in the direction of the light, I gave the buckskin his head, hoping he had the strength to pick his way across the broken ground. A mountain-bred pony, he was very good at this under normal circumstances.

Now I could feel him shuddering beneath me, not frightened of the trail, but simply exhausted. I forced him to continue into the depths of the canyon where deep shadows spread themselves across our path. The buckskin slipped once, twice on the shale underfoot, but we continued on. Exiting the canyon mouth the buckskin lifted his head suddenly, and by moonlight I saw his ears prick. Could it be that he smelled water, heard others of his kind in the distance?

I did not hold him back, but did not hurry him either as we crossed a flat where salt grass and ocotillo grew. He seemed sure of his destination now. I actually found myself having to slow the big animal.

Then I saw the light again. A solitary beacon. I did not know who I might meet, what sort of welcome awaited me. It no longer mattered. If I could only have a few sips of water before I died.

We emerged from the canyon shadows to find a level patch of ground

surrounding a pole-and-adobe struc-
ture about the size of an outbuilding
standing alone on that treeless, lifeless
soil. There was a light flickering dimly
through a slit window and I guided
the buckskin toward it. His head was
still lifted eagerly, but as we neared the
shanty his front knees buckled and he
rolled, throwing me to the ground.

My head struck rock and the world
began to spin crazily, the night stars
spiraling away madly, the mocking
moon staring down at me from the
long, lonely desert sky before all went
dark and silent and life seem to shatter
into meaningless fragments with no
consciousness left to hold it together.

★   ★   ★

When I came to, nothing fit right. I was
on my back somewhere, but sheltered.
A fiercely blinding ray of new sunlight
streamed through a slot in the shelter
and stung my eyes with its fury as if I
were an ancient enemy deserving to be

blinded. My head ached savagely, and I could not remember why that should be so.

Stranger still was the spectre I saw mumbling and pacing the floor, cutting off the light and then allowing it to carve its saberlike way through the rough walls. Remembering a little of what had happened, I tried to sit up. Failing that I fell back again, fists clenched. I thought first of the buckskin horse.

'Is my horse dead?' I asked in a voice that was not mine and was scarcely human. The spectre stopped its pacing.

It spoke. 'No. He'll outlive you. If you don't have some powerful explanations. We don't hang men for murder out here. We just shoot them.'

Had my past caught up with me then? How could anyone in this desolate territory know who I was? I understood none of it. My shadowy host crossed the narrow room and jerked my head up, spilling some of the contents of his canteen into my mouth.

Roughly he let my head again drop on to the bunk where I had been placed and resumed his pacing.

'I'm not a murderer,' I managed to say through my sun-blistered lips.

'No?'

'You see in Flagstaff . . . '

'Damn Flagstaff! Tell me what happened to Ray Hardin and why you were carrying his wallet!'

2

I rubbed my encrusted eyes and tried to sit up again. I made it halfway and, leaning on my elbows, I watched as the spectre emerged from the heavy shadows, cut across that beam of harsh daylight and approached me again. Now I saw a narrow-built man of an age somewhere between fifty and a hundred wearing twill trousers held up by a pair of red suspenders looped over his scrawny shoulders. He had a thinning patch of silver hair on his knobby head and a squint in one eye. He also had a rifle in his hands — my rifle. He was not smiling.

'Are you going to tell me, or aren't you?' he asked in a scratchy voice.

'I'll tell you. How about another drink of water.'

He shook his head from side to side slowly, definitely. 'Tell me your story first. I might just be wasting water.' He had raised the muzzle of the Winchester so that I could look into its dark bore.

I told him slowly, carefully what had happened back at Coyote Wells. He listened patiently but dubiously.

'I didn't want to leave his wallet and papers out there,' I told him. 'What would be the point in giving them up to the desert sands?'

'Did you bury Ray proper?' the old man demanded.

'I didn't have the strength, Friend. Besides, as I told you, there were Yaquis prowling around the Wells.'

Thoughtfully he said, 'Well, I guess maybe you did all that you could do. If you're telling the truth.'

'I am. I never even knew Ray Hardin. What would I kill him for?'

He pondered that, again withdrawing a little into the shadows of the tiny cabin. 'Did you see his horse? Big bay?'

'No. I've told you all I saw out there. The Yaquis didn't have his horse either. They were afoot when I saw them.'

' 'Spect Art Corson stole it. Funny he didn't search Ray's body and take his wallet.'

'Maybe the Yaquis spooked them. Or they saw me coming and thought I might be trouble. Is there anything valuable in the wallet?'

'It wouldn't be to most people,' he shrugged. 'Don't concern yourself about it anyway.' He propped my rifle in a corner of the room, went to the puncheon table where the canteen lay and tossed it to me. I uncorked it and took a long pull of water. The old man stood staring out the slot window, hands on his hips.

'Who's Beth?' I asked him.

He turned sharply toward me, his profile stark and set in silhouette. 'I thought we agreed you weren't going to concern yourself with Ray's business.'

'I guess we did,' I muttered, lying back again. And, I thought, as I stared up at the ceiling, I did not need to concern myself with any other business than getting across the Colorado River and into California. Not with the law riding behind me. Why then did I still feel the nagging tug of guilt about the promise I had made to Ray Hardin as he lay dying? I shook the thought aside and somehow again fell asleep.

It was near dusk when I awoke. The shadows had shifted; the sun no longer cut harshly through the narrow window. The old man was gone. That was my intention as well. I couldn't stay where I was even had I been welcome. Not knowing whether or not Sheriff Tom Driscoll was on my trail. I had to find my buckskin horse and assess his condition. If I could ride on, now was the time to do it, with the cool of evening beginning to settle. And if the horse had foundered — well, I would just have to take a shot at walking my way across Arizona Territory.

Getting up from the cot was trickier than I could have imagined. My head reeled as I sat up, and I had to pause to gather my strength before attempting to rise to my feet. I needed food, more water, rest. I had none of these. I looked in vain for the canteen, but the old man had taken it with him, wherever he had gone. Ray Hardin's wallet was on the table, still apparently unopened. I started to toss it aside and then, on impulse, pocketed it with the vague idea that I would glance through it and see if there was some sort of address there and then mail the contents to whoever it might concern in Yuma once I was safely out of the Territory. I was willing to do that much at least to fulfill my promise to the dead man.

I was a little surprised to find my Winchester still propped up in the corner of the cabin. Gratefully I snatched it up and checked the loads. I made my way to the door and swung it open, squinting into the distances. I rested one hand against the jamb and stood taking in a few steadying deep breaths before I made my heavy way into the dusky yard.

The sky had faded to deep crimson.

There was a pleasing carpet of purple sand verbena spread spottily across the ground, a thicket of nopal cactus and one lonesome ocotillo, its spiny coachman's whips undecorated by vermilion flowers at this time of year. There was not a tree anywhere. I smiled thinly. When was the last time I had seen a tree of any kind?

I found the buckskin, unsaddled, standing in the scant shade of a brush lean-to. There was no other horse there. But the lean-to was evidence that the old man did have a mount. That meant that he had taken it and intended to travel some distance. The buckskin lifted its muzzle from the fodder it had been given and glanced at me woefully.

I ran my hands over his legs and flanks. Despite ill-usage he seemed sound if not up to strength. It was with regret that I searched for my saddle and horse blanket and prepared to ride. I wasted little time. For all I knew the old man had gone to find help and would return with more trouble for me. I did not wish to be there when he arrived. Swinging aboard the weary buckskin horse I turned his head westward, toward California, through the purpling dusk.

The day was still warm, but the devil winds had subsided. The shadows stretched out long and deep before the dull glow of sundown. The land here was barren, littered with small reddish volcanic stones. Now and then there would be patches of drift sand, but the land was flat and the travel relatively easy. There were more saguaro now and stands of jumping cactus — cholla. To the south I could see a phantom glow of light which I took to be Yuma. I was not far from the Colorado River then.

Yuma could not have existed without the river. It was the last stop-over for water before the pioneers crossed to the Mojave Desert on the California side. I was well aware that there was no easy travel across that region either. In earlier times a few expeditions had tried following a new trail farther to the north, guided by the rumor that there was easier passage there. These travelers were the ones that had given Death Valley its name.

Yuma had one more reason for existing. Yuma Territorial Prison where the true hard cases were sent to be locked away in its vaults. They had chosen Yuma because although the prison might not be absolutely escape-proof, once a prisoner was on the run there was nowhere to go but out on to the desert where, beneath a cruel sun, the wilderness issued its own sort of death warrant.

The buckskin was moving easily beneath me, though not at his usual jaunty pace. The night settled in quickly, bringing that brief moment of comfort between the searing heat of day and the frigid temperatures of night. I had my rifle and my pony. Sheriff Tom Driscoll, if he was following me, was well behind and, anyway, with any luck I would be across the Colorado River and into California, out of his jurisdiction, by daybreak.

I should have been breathing in a fresh sense of freedom with each passing mile.

Why then did I slow my horse, halt it and look over my shoulder toward the distant glow of Yuma's lights?

Well, I knew why, but it was a foolish way of thinking.

A rash promise made to a dying man who would never know that I hadn't lived up to my word, who could no longer even care. I regretted taking the wallet from the cabin. The old man seemed to know who Beth was. Maybe he could have delivered it to her. I had never even learned his name. For all I knew the old man was, himself, this Corson who had murdered Ray Hardin. I took off my hat and ran my fingers through my damp, longish hair. The buckskin shuddered impatiently beneath me, now eager to be going on.

Who was Beth? I wondered. A grieving widow, a lover, a friend, a little girl waiting for her daddy to return? Was there a last letter to someone in Ray Hardin's wallet, something of great sentimental value, important news, some notification of prayed-for good fortune, a mortgage paper on some land or shop long-labored to obtain? What made any of it my business? Only a careless promise made to soften a man's departure from this world.

I had my own life to worry about. They would be happy to stretch my neck for me back in Flagstaff, guilty or not, if Tom Driscoll caught up with me. I much preferred to go on living a little longer. I replaced my hat and sat brooding in the saddle as full dark crept into the skies and the brilliant desert stars blinked on one by one. The buckskin impatiently shifted his hoofs once more. I turned his head with my reins and muttered.

'Let's go. Change of plans.' And started making my way toward the lights of Yuma. 'Horse — you can tell the world that John Magadan is purely a fool.'

By the time I reached the outskirts of Yuma the moon was riding high once more, silver against the black velvet sky. I passed a sign that read 'Pop, 1240' — I assumed that didn't include the prisoners locked up in the penitentiary. That made Yuma a not inconsiderable-sized town in the West, although people in the East or St. Louis, say, might view it as a fly speck on the map. The point is, that Yuma was of size enough so that I couldn't walk down the street rapping on doors, hoping to find someone named Beth, not even knowing who she was.

The best approach to the dilemma seemed to be finding anyone who might know Ray Hardin. Hostlers, bartenders, inn-keepers. The town, though large by desert standards, was still small enough that if Hardin had lived for very long in Yuma I would eventually find someone who recognized the name and could lead me to Beth.

The buckskin had done well by me, as well as he could. The first thing to do was to see that he was sheltered, watered and fed. I hadn't a dime in my pockets, though, and I frowned at that thought as I sat the quivering horse in the deep shadows of a shuttered hardware store on the outskirts of town.

For the first time I opened Ray Hardin's wallet and thumbed through its contents. Tucked away in one corner of its fold was a yellow-back ten-dollar note, and I slipped it out. I did not feel like a thief. I was employing Ray Hardin's resources for the job he had asked me to do.

Besides, from what I understand of matters, Ray no longer had much use for that ten-dollar bill.

It was too dark to glance through the papers the wallet contained, and the horse was impatient as any thirsty animal might be, and so I let him walk on down the silent street, searching for a stable.

On the far side of town I could hear the distance-muffled sounds of loud celebrations. That was where the saloons would be, grouped together away from the decent folks of Yuma.

That might be a good place to start asking about Hardin, although I did not know what kind of man he had been. He may have never entered a saloon in his life.

Nor did I know if he had enemies other than Corson. I might be mentioning a name that would bring more trouble down on my head. What was I doing here! I could have reached the river by now, been free of cares. I shook my head wondering at my own stupidity.

The stable I found was dark, silent except for the nickering of a single horse in the back of the establishment. I swung down anyway, leading the buckskin to the big double doors. It was uncommon for a stable to be without a watchman ever. People arrived at odd hours from the westward trail. People stole horses at any hour. I halted in the open doorway and called in. After a minute a thin, irritated voice answered.

'Comin'. I'm comin'.'

When the stablehand emerged from

the depths of the building I found a doughy, stubby man with a wide chest whose squeaky voice did not match his bulk. His eyes were red with sleep. He was annoyed and I couldn't blame him much. He eyed me and then studied the buckskin more closely, a man who obviously knew much about horses.

'About run him down to the nub, didn't you?' he asked, feeling the buckskin's hocks for tell-tale heat.

'It's a long dry trail from Tucson,' I said. Still he gave me a look of disgust for treating the noble animal so badly.

'What do you want to give him? Alfalfa and a few scoops of oats is what I'd recommend.'

'That sounds right. I'll trust your judgement. You seem to be a man who knows your horses.'

''Course I know my horses!' the hostler said with a flare of temper. 'What do I do day and night, night and day?'

I had to smile inwardly at his attitude, but I was happy to see the buckskin in the hands of a man who not only knew animals, but cared about them.

'I'd go easy on the water at first.' I said. 'He hasn't had a full belly for a while.'

The stable man didn't even bother to respond to that. He gave me a sort of pitying glance, the sort a professional gives an amateur instructing him in how to go about his job.

'Fifty cents a day,' is what he said. 'You want to tote that rifle around town with you or not? I've got a chain rack over on the wall there. Never lost a weapon yet.'

I glanced that way and saw the gunrack with a thin chain passing through the lever-actions of half a dozen rifles.

'I'll leave the rifle,' I agreed.

'Ten cents more.'

'All right.' I paused as he began to unfasten the double cinches on my Texas-rigged saddle, then asked him, 'Do you know a man named Ray

Hardin? He's an old friend of mine. I heard he lives down this way.'

He didn't look up as he answered. 'Mister, I know where you can get a meal or a drink. I can tell you where the town marshal's office is, or the hotel. Outside of that — I know nothing at all.' He swung my saddle on to the stall partition, whipped off the buckskin's blanket and began to curry the horse. I guessed our conversation was at an end.

The streets were cool, but not frigid like the open desert. I supposed the wooden buildings absorbed heat through-out the day and gave it off again in the night. I shivered a little nevertheless as I stood in front of the stable, looking up and down the street. I was hungry and thirsty and weary to the bone. I did, however, have ten dollars of Ray Hardin's money, and with any luck at all I would awake in the morning a stronger, well-rested man.

First I started uptown toward the sound of the saloon crowds. I wanted to begin my search as quickly as possible because I had no intention of remaining long in Yuma. I am not a drinking man, but my throat and deprived body agreed that a tall beer would go far toward assuaging some of my lingering exhaustion.

And I had it in mind to ask around about Ray Hardin. Someone must have known the man. *Someone* must know who Beth was and how I could find her to rid myself of the burden of conscience I was carrying, and ride for the Colorado River and freedom. I was still unsteady on my feet. I cursed my own body as I had to pause not once but twice and lean against the fronts of buildings while I made my way across town. The silver moon still hung high in the night sky, still mocked my smallness. The shadows were deep before the false-front buildings along the street I now walked. A spotted dog stirred and scuttled away, tail between its legs. I passed one man and then another, neither showing any interest in a wandering stranger.

I emerged on to a lighted avenue where dozens of cowhands, soldiers, drifters and whatnots stood in front of a dozen saloons swapping stories, bragging, cat-calling to each other. I entered the first establishment I came to through green-painted batwing doors, and settled at the far end of the bar, leaning my forearms on its scarred surface, my hat tilted back on my head. I looked no rougher than half of the men in the noisy saloon, and the big-chested bartender served me a beer without comment.

The beer was tall, tepid, flat and wonderfully reviving. The tissues of my body seemed to be sparring each with the others for their own share. My eyes seemed to cool, my dizziness began to pass. As it did, I felt the beginnings of hunger growing. I could not recall my last meal.

The man with the shaggy red beard nudged my shoulder as he eased up to the bar, apologized, put his hat on the counter and called for a whisky. He slapped a silver dollar on the bar, and nodding at me, told the bartender. 'I'll pay for his as well.'

'Never saw you here before,' he said, tossing down his whisky in one gulp. He had a pleasant if crooked smile, wore a faded red shirt and black jeans tucked into run-down boots.

'Just rode in,' I answered. 'Thanks for the beer.'

He nodded and asked me no more questions. He signaled to the bartender for another whisky. I decided to take a chance and said:

'I've got some business with a man named Ray Hardin. Only thing is, I can't find him.'

'Ray Hardin!' the man laughed. 'You just haven't been looking hard enough, friend. I could spit on his house from here. Let me point you toward it.'

He was still smiling, maybe because he was in a drunken-friendly mood, I don't know. With his heavy arm across my shoulders we wove our way through the crowd of drinkers to the back door of the saloon. I stepped out into the darkness with him.

'You see that white house across the vacant lot?' he asked pointing. And when I nodded he laughed out loud and said, 'Well, Ray Hardin don't live there!' and he threw a heavy punch at me. His fist landed solidly on the hinge of my jaw, and I staggered back against the wall of the saloon. When he hit me again I went to my knees in the dark alley. When he kicked my head I went down to stay.

3

'What the hell happened to you?' a deep voice was demanding of me. A rough hand shook my shoulder, and I opened my eyes to look up at the dark skies and the man with the silver star pinned to his leather vest standing over me. 'Somebody beat you up?' the lawman wanted to know. He crouched down beside me and peered at my face.

'No,' I groaned. The last thing I wanted was to be interviewed by a marshal. I could not give my name; I could not refuse to. 'I guess I got a little drunk,' I said sheepishly. 'Must have fallen and banged myself up a little.

The lawman stood, considering me. He probably didn't believe me, but officers in these Western towns don't have much time to waste with common drunks. After a moment's thought, he ordered me:

'In that case just get yourself to bed somewhere. We can't have people passed-out in the alleys. And don't go back into that saloon!' he warned me. 'Then I will have to run you in.'

I rose from the ground unsteadily and leaned my back against the wall. My head was ringing and I clutched my temples with both hands. The lawman seemed convinced by now that I was just one more man who couldn't hold his liquor. He picked up my hat and handed it to me.

'Remember what I said — don't come back here tonight.'

'No, sir,' I answered quietly. I turned and started unsteadily away, feeling nausea and anger rise simultaneously. I would have liked to go back and find the red-bearded man, but that could only lead to more trouble, quite serious trouble for me if they discovered I was an escaped murderer.

I was making a poor job of the search for Beth.

At the head of the alley in the silence

of the night, I leaned against yet another building and patted my pockets. Ray Hardin's wallet was gone! Cursing myself for my own carelessness, I stood there for a moment, breathing the night air in deeply. The scent of sage was heavy and I could smell water across the desert's breadth. The Colorado River, no doubt.

I could recover the buckskin now, this minute, and ride toward California. It was the wisest thing I could have done. Instead I searched my jeans and found the much-folded ten-dollar note in the watch pocket, and started off to look for a place to sleep.

★ ★ ★

The window of my hotel room faced west and so without the morning sun to awaken me I slept late, dreaming the dreams of the dead. I stood at the morning window looking out across the length of Yuma toward the vast desert distances. I could not see the

41

tombs of the Territorial Prison from there, for which I was grateful. I raised the window a bit and the warm desert breeze caused the thin white curtains to flutter.

I felt stiff. Weary. There were a few new lumps on my head. But somehow I felt happier. I was off the desert; I had enough money in my pocket to buy a real breakfast; my horse was being well-tended to. It wasn't much, and I had come into a new set of troubles, but a man can't have everything. I was certainly better off than I had been the day before.

I opened the door to my room and sat on the bed. After a minute or two I saw a young blond kid with a towel over his forearm and a ceramic basin in his hands scurrying along the corridor. I gestured to him and told him that I would be grateful for some warm water, a bar of soap, and a razor. Contemplating that made me feel even better. A shave, a quick wash down, breakfast. The day seemed to be growing brighter with each passing minute.

I sensed rather than saw her enter the room and I rose abruptly.

'I hear you've been trying to find me,' she said. 'I'm Beth.'

Young, blue-eyed, her ears were small and set flat against her skull, her mouth was full, especially the underlip. Her hair was of the shade they call strawberry-blond. It was pinned up under a tiny, tilted blue cap. She wore a dark blue dress of the sort I can't describe except to say it had ruffles at the throat and at the cuffs.

'How did you know I was looking for you?' I asked.

'Henry Tyler rode in to tell me,' she said, meaning I supposed, the old man in whose cabin I had stayed. She closed the door behind her. 'Now I'll have it!'

From the folds of her skirt she withdrew a small silver-plated .40 caliber derringer, and quite deliberately aimed it in my direction. Her mouth was set, her pretty eyes determined. I automatically raised my hands. I tried a smile that didn't make any impression at all.

'Lady — Beth — I don't know what in *hell* you're talking about.'

'Don't use that sort of language to me,' she ordered. 'You know where it is. Henry said that Ray gave you his wallet. If you don't have it, who does?'

'It's the wallet you're after?' I asked. I lowered my hands. She didn't seem to mind that, but her little derringer didn't waver and the expression in her eyes did not change. 'Look . . . ' I took a step toward her.

'Stay where you are. I'll fire, and if you are thinking this pistol can't do some damage, try it.'

I wasn't thinking that. A derringer was probably the most inaccurate weapon ever devised with its little inch and a half barrel. But it held two .40 caliber slugs, and many a gambler had discovered that across a card table it could do its deadly work quite well. We were only about that distance apart.

The dry wind gusted, blowing the curtains farther into the room. There was a sharp rap on the door.

'Who's that?' Beth asked without shifting her eyes.

'Probably the house boy with hot water and soap. I asked him to bring some up to me.'

'All right.' She sidled to the corner of the room. 'Answer the door. You look like you could use soap and water.'

Under the watch of the twin muzzles of the derringer I opened the door. It was the boy, as I had guessed. He handed me the basin, soap and razor and flipped a fresh towel over my shoulder. He lingered, waiting for a tip, I suppose, but I had no change to give him. I heeled the door shut and walked to the small dresser against the far wall where I placed the basin and towel down. The oval mirror attached to the dresser began to fog slowly from the water's heat. I turned to Beth for further orders.

'Go ahead, wash up. You need it.'

45

'I'll be taking my shirt off,' I warned her.

She didn't reply, just sat in the wooden chair in the far corner with that little pistol in her lap. I stripped off my shirt and washed up, then lathered my face with the bar soap provided and began to shave.

There was another knock at the door, and I glanced that way by way of the mirror. I saw Beth rise expectantly and step toward the door without hesitation. Now what? The door was quickly opened and rapidly shut behind the newcomer. I knew him. It was Henry Tyler, in whose cabin I had spent the night. He held a Winchester rifle, wore a flop hat, a white shirt and his red suspenders.

'What has he told you?' I heard him ask Beth in a low voice.

'Nothing yet.'

They both sat — Beth again on the wooden chair, the old man on the bed, the rifle across his lap. I eyed the Winchester closely, if it wasn't my own rifle, it was its twin. I finished shaving and shrugged into my dusty blue shirt. I had to ask them:

'Do you mind telling me what's going on, what you want of me?'

It was Tyler who answered. 'Ray Hardin's wallet. What did you do with it?'

'It got lifted from me,' I told him, briefly describing the incident in the alley behind the saloon.

'This man . . . what did he look like?' Tyler asked, scratching at his chin. I described the bearded man as well as I could and Tyler's frown deepened.

He shook his head as if I was the world's greatest fool. 'It was McQueen,' he commented, to Beth. 'One of Art Corson's men,' he explained to me.

'Look,' I said wearily. 'I don't know what trouble you people have. I don't know Corson or McQueen. I don't want anything from you, and I have nothing that would be of any help to you. I found Ray Hardin as he was dying. I promised him that I would tell

47

Beth that he had tried to do his best. I had his wallet. Then I got it taken from me. That's all there is to it!' I told them, growing a little exasperated. 'Plus, I haven't had a meal of any kind in two days. You'd be surprised how important that is becoming to me. Leave here, will you? Or let me go on my way.'

'Breakfast is taken care of,' Tyler said evenly. 'I ordered it on my way up to your room. The boy will deliver it shortly.' I took a step toward him and he whispered, 'Sit down if you don't want to be shot.'

The room had only the single chair and Beth, her eyes as fierce as ever, had seated herself there. Henry Tyler was perched on the bed, and so I leaned against the wall and lowered myself to the floor, folding my hands between my knees, wondering again what I had gotten myself into. And more — wondering how to get out of it.

I saw Beth's blue eyes flicker, saw a little light appear in their depths then fade, saw a nearly undetectable smile twitch at one corner of her pretty mouth. She said to Tyler, 'I think I understand a little better now, Henry. Why was he riding the desert alone, without water and poorly provisioned? Why did he take Ray Hardin's wallet? I think we have a man on the run here. What did he tell you at your cabin?'

Tyler lifted his eyes to me, remembering. 'I accused him of being a murderer — Ray's killer. Then he said a strange thing. I can't remember his exact words, but it was to the effect that he was no murderer, and that he was innocent of what had happened in Flagstaff.'

'He's a man on the run,' Beth said with a little satisfied nod. 'He'll help us now or find himself in prison.' She smiled again, and for a pretty girl it was a brutal expression. 'What is it you're wanted for, Magadan? Robbery, horse-stealing, cattle-rustling?'

'Murder,' I told her quietly, and the little lady, tough as she appeared, seemed to blanch on hearing the harsh word.

Once more there was a knock on the door. 'That'll be your breakfast,' Tyler said rising.

It was. I sat cross-legged on the floor eating four eggs, hotcakes, hominy, ham and biscuits, following it with three cups of coffee. Not a word passed between them as I devoured the food. They watched silently, with distant interest as if I were some creature in a zoo cage.

As I ate I considered many things. Who were these people? What did they want of me? Could I reach the window and leap on to the balcony, drop to the street before they shot me? Would they shoot?

As I placed my dishes aside, Tyler spoke as if he had been reading my thoughts. 'You can't afford to try anything, Magadan. Your own words have given you away. You're an escaped murderer. If we have to shoot you — well,' he shrugged, 'it's not even a crime. It's more a citizen's duty to eliminate men like you.'

I didn't respond to that. It was true enough. I finished the last of my coffee and asked, 'What is it you people want of me?'

'We need the *number*. If you don't know what it is, we have to go after Corson and his two friends and get it from them. The two of us aren't equipped to handle the job. Sorry if it hurts your feelings to say this, Beth, but it's true. We're only one small girl and an old man. You, Magadan, on the other hand, are young and strong. There's no one else — not in Yuma — that we can trust.'

It seemed to me that he was talking in circles. I didn't have an idea what he wanted, except that he meant for me to go out on to the cruel desert once again and try to track down this Art Corson.

'No,' I said flatly. 'I've spent a week trying to escape the desert. I'll not go out on to it again.'

'Beth?' Tyler said. 'You know where the town marshal's office is.'

She rose from her chair, and I was

forced to motion her to take her seat again. 'You aren't giving me much choice, are you?'

'No. I'm trying not to,' Henry Tyler said.

'My horse is beat up.'

'That big buckskin of yours had a rest at my cabin and spent last night in a comfortable stable.'

'I'd have to go over and . . . '

'That's taken care of. He's hitched out front. Water bags on the saddle horn. The hotel bill's been paid. All you have to do is swing aboard and we're on our way.'

'The girl. How can she possibly ride with us on a trek like this?' I ran an exasperated hand over my head, pointing at the petite woman in her little tilted hat and wide blue skirts.

'It'll be all right,' Tyler said calmly.

'Look out the window, Magadan,' Beth ordered, and I got to my feet, frustrated, confused and angry. Would these people really turn me over to the law, see me hung? I had the feeling that they were capable of it. The sky outside my window was blue-white. Two men who seemed to be miners or prospectors passed by on the nearly deserted street below, riding mules, leading another laden with supplies. I heard the rustling of material and finally turned around to see Beth, her dress kicked aside, standing there in blue jeans and a white blouse which she must have been wearing under her outer garments all the time.

'Will you do one thing for me?' I asked, my eyes shuttling from Henry Tyler's to Beth's. 'Just give me an idea of what in hell is going on!'

Beth's frown signaled that she was about to — once again — lecture me about my language.

Tyler looked to Beth. 'The man is correct. He does have a right to know what has happened.' He rubbed his knobby forehead and then smoothed down his wispy silver hair. He withdrew a brass pocket watch from his trousers, glanced at it and said, 'But not here.

Not now. We have to be getting on our way.'

The morning sun was still low enough so that the temperature was comfortable when we emerged from the hotel on to the dry streets of Yuma. Sure enough my tall buckskin horse was standing at the hitch rail, two waterbags hung from the pommel of my saddle, one on either side. I pulled my hat lower over my eyes and swung aboard, leather creaking under my weight. Hitched alongside my horse were a slender-legged little blue roan and a stocky sorrel about twelve years old. Henry Tyler gave the girl a hand up on to the blue roan and mounted the sorrel and we started out of Yuma along the dusty street.

Noon found us in a cottonwood grove where a slender silver rill wove its way southward to join the Colorado River. The shade beneath the wind-fluttered cottonwood trees shifted with each gust of wind. Along the creek cicadas murmured to one another and a group of iridescent blue and orange dragonflies skimmed back and forth across the stream. The horses were led to water and drank, from time to time lifting water-silvered muzzles to glance at us and the land around us.

It was dry and still, quiet except for the insect noises and the wind whispering through the trees. Tyler had given my rifle back to me, but I knew by its heft that he had unloaded it. I shoved it into my saddle scabbard with a natural-enough resentment. I was, in fact a prisoner to these two.

'I need a full explanation,' I said roughly. I was leaning against the shoulder of my buckskin horse, arms folded. 'Threats won't hold me long.'

'We didn't think so,' Henry Tyler said in response. 'If it weren't so important . . . '

'I'll tell him, Henry,' Beth said quietly. 'So that he'll understand why we're doing this.'

She walked slowly away from me, toward the darker shade of the

55

cottonwood grove. She glanced back at me over her shoulder, and, shrugging, I followed her.

Twenty or thirty feet on, Beth stopped and seated herself on the waist-high branch of a mottled cottonwood tree. She was a pleasing sight sitting there in the scattered shade in her jeans and white blouse, the wind teasing her light hair, but I carried my frown successfully.

'You'd better start from the beginning and give me a good reason to stay, Beth. I'm a troubled man and I need no more of this. Much as I'd hate to do it, if I have to crack Henry over the head and make my way to California, I will.'

'You don't understand,' she said in a voice that was softer than I had heard from her before. 'We need you! Badly.'

I seated myself on the low hanging bough beside her, removed my hat and waited, glancing now and then at her lovely profile. She sighed; her hands fluttered in the air.

'It's all about Ben, of course,' she

told me, leaving me no more enlightened than before.

'You're going to have to flesh out these remarks, Beth. I have no idea who 'Ben' is.'

'Ben Tolliver, of course! My brother.'

'All right,' I answered calmly. She was obviously agitated. I knew she would get around to telling me the whole story eventually, and so I waited. It's not always easy to speak of painful matters.

'My brother, Ben, is serving time in the Territorial Prison for crimes he did not commit,' Beth told me. 'Stop!' she raised her hand. 'I know that's what all prisoners say, but proof exists that he is innocent. I know where it is, I just can't get to it.'

'Is that where all this business with Ray Hardin comes in?'

'Yes, it is. Have you ever heard of the Pulver Gang?'

'Sure. Bank robbers, killers.'

'Well, Ben fell in with them — in a way. He had a small horse ranch and sold stock to them. He didn't know who they were, what they did, only that they paid top-dollar for their mounts.'

'I take it that the judge and jury didn't believe that,' I said.

'No. But there is proof that Ben was railroaded, that the gang used him for a fall guy after a murder was done.'

'What sort of proof?' I asked.

'The gang broke up eventually. I don't know the exact reason, but Jefferson Pulver and this man Corson had a falling out. Corson shot his former leader. While Pulver was lying on his death bed he dictated a letter, naming names, exposing facts.'

'Including the fact that your brother was not guilty of murder?'

'Yes. Pulver wrote Ben a letter telling him that he would be exonerated once the confession was made public.'

'Corson didn't like the idea, I take it.'

'Of course not! It was Corson who did the murder. Ben told me so.'

'I don't quite understand this. Why hide the confession? Why didn't Jefferson Pulver call the law to his deathbed and tell them all of this?'

Beth gave me a pitying look as if I had rocks for brains. 'Don't you see? The officers of the law were all on the take in Flagstaff. I thought you of all people would understand that Sheriff Tom Driscoll is corrupt enough to lock anyone up, even hang a man, so long as Corson was paying him off.'

Tom Driscoll? No, I hadn't known, but now many things began to make sense. How I had been sentenced to hang for killing a man when I hadn't been in miles of his camp. Perhaps I did deserve the critical look Beth Tolliver was giving me. Perhaps I *did* have rocks for brains.

Beth was saying something else that I didn't get. My attention was elsewhere. She paused, pushed aside an errant strand of pale hair and frowned at me again.

'But you're not even listening to me,' she said with a shadow of petulance.

She was right. I had been listening to the slow, stealthy approach of horses in the near-distance.

Without ceremony I rose, yanked her off the tree bough by her wrist and started running back toward the stream where we had left Henry Tyler. Stumbling, struggling in my grip she shouted angrily:

'What are you doing!'

'We have to get to Henry. I need my rifle, and I need it loaded! Now!'

4

It was close. We found Henry, shirtless, rinsing off in the stream. I shouted to him, grabbed my Winchester and instinctively he understood the urgency in my words. He ran to his saddlebags and tossed me a box of .44-40s. I was still thumbing the brass cartridges into the tube magazine when the raiders broke from the cottonwoods across the creek. I shoved Beth roughly to the ground, went to a knee and levered a round into the breech of the needle-gun.

There were four of them and they charged at us across the narrow rill, their horses' hoofs sending up silver fans of water. I guessed that I had loaded ten shots, and that should have been enough. But then I saw Henry Tyler, bare-chested still, gunned down before he could bring his revolver to bear.

Smothering an oath I shot the man who had killed him, watching as he flung out his arms and dropped from his horse's back into the shallow rill. Switching my sights I aimed two rapid shots at the man to his left. He, I recognized. McQueen's flowing red beard flowed wildly past his throat as his horse charged. My bullet caught him just below his chin, and he slumped forward across his pony's withers. The horse reared up and bucked him from the saddle. He lay still on the sandy bank as the other two outlaws rode for cover.

I motioned to Beth to stay down and scooted to one side to my buckskin's flank for protection while I scanned the cottonwood grove for signs of movement.

For half an hour, perhaps, I remained there, crouched beside my horse, but I heard no sounds and saw no movement in the shadows of the scattered trees.

'I think it's all right now,' I whispered to Beth.

'You can't be sure.'

'No, I can't be sure, but we can't stay here. They may come back.'

'We have to bury the dead,' Beth said, holding her fingertips to her mouth.

'There's three of them,' I said more roughly than I intended, tightening the cinches on my saddle. 'There isn't time.'

'No, I suppose not,' she answered reluctantly.

'Look — is this Corson?' I asked, toeing the second bandit over. She shuddered visibly and turned away after a brief glimpse.

'I have no idea what Corson looks like. Only . . . only Henry did.'

I squatted down beside the man I knew to be McQueen and went through his pockets. I found what I was looking for. With an inappropriate grin I rose and held Ray Hardin's wallet up for Beth to see. 'Still had it on him.'

'Yes.' Her voice was thin; her face was bloodless. 'Can we go now?'

Gathering up the lead to Henry Tyler's sorrel, I swung aboard the buckskin and we started away from the river, leaving the blessed shade of the cottonwoods behind. The sky was high and harsh. I was grateful to Tyler for the waterbags he had had sense enough to bring along. The desert was as long and desolate as ever. A gathering of vultures began to soar on high, forming a dark, tragic image. Beth saw them but kept her eyes averted.

A mile or so on she said, 'Surely we're going in the wrong direction.'

I reined up briefly. Her blue eyes were clear despite the blistering sun. She looked as if she had just stepped out of her bath. A few wisps of pale hair had slipped down from the fawn-colored Stetson she wore to drift across her forehead. I wanted to speak softly to her, but I had to make myself clear and so my voice was a little rough.

'Listen, Beth. I don't know what you two had in mind when you roped me into this, but I am not going to chase after Corson, am not about to go back to Flagstaff where they have a hangman's noose waiting for me. I've chosen this direction to get as far away as possible from the men who want to gun us down, from the men who killed Henry Tyler.'

'You're afraid of them.'

'Damn right.'

She didn't criticize my language, though for a moment I thought she was going to actually cry and that made me feel more like a heel than ever. We rode for ten or more silent miles before I halted again, scanning the far horizon and said, 'Let's swing down and give these horses a break. It'll soon be dark. No one can sneak up on us on these flats.'

I had it in mind to rest the horses, to apologize, then continue on our way in the morning. Except it wasn't *our* way. I was determined to make California. She was dead-set on reaching Flagstaff and finding proof of her brother's innocence. It didn't look as if I was going to be able to talk her out of it. I didn't like the idea of a woman trying to cross that expanse of desert on her own, with known killers and bands of Yaqui Indians roaming the trackless wasteland, but what was I to do?

No sooner had she swung down from her blue roan's back than she stuck out her hand and said, 'Let me see Ray Hardin's wallet, please.'

With evening descending the breeze had risen. Crouched down Beth began to go through the billfold, removing every scrap of paper, weighting them down with pebbles to keep them from being blown away. Every piece of paper was spread out before her; her frown only deepened. A hint of despair had crept into her eyes.

'What is it we're looking for?' I asked, squatting beside her.

'The number!' she said as if I were the idiot of the world.

'Look,' I said, moderating my voice. 'That's the second time you've told me that we are looking for a number that is important. Thing is — excuse me — I have no idea what you're talking about.'

We were speaking in those few graceful twilight desert hours with the sky in the west reddening, the heat of the day dissipating. Doves winged past overhead, cutting quick 'V's as they made their way toward their secret watering places. The crimson sky painted the desert to deep red and violet. Beth's cheeks were flushed with the evening light. She had removed her broad-brimmed hat and it hung down her neck by a rawhide string, letting her hair drift in the breeze. She was a pretty picture at that moment as the long desert, transformed itself from hell to a landscape of muted beauty.

Wearily, Beth said: 'I told you that Jefferson Pulver had written a full confession on his death bed. Probably after he and Corson had a falling-out, he wanted to make sure that his former friend got his.'

'So you said.'

'The confession is locked in a safety

deposit box in a Flagstaff bank. That's what he wrote to my brother in his letter of apology. I need to be able to open it.'

'You don't have the key? Is that it?'

'Do I not!' Beth said. She reached into the neck of her blouse and showed me a brass key hanging from a chain. 'You didn't go through Ray Hardin's wallet, but Henry did. He found the key and rode to Yuma to give it to me.'

'Then . . . ?'

'Then we don't know the box number!' Beth said in frustration. 'The bank is not going to let me go in and try fitting my key into every safety deposit box in its building. Can you imagine how its other customers would feel about that!'

'I see.' Dusk was settling and her face was fading away from me. Now twin rivulets of tears silvered her cheeks. 'But Ray Hardin knew the number? Is that it?'

'Yes,' her muted voice whispered out of the gloaming. She sighed, leaned back with her hands between her knees and explained. 'You'd have to have known Ray. He was a former Texas Ranger with a lot of expertise in various areas. Well,' she waved a fluttering hand, 'I told Ray my problem and . . . and I guess he was courting me and I let him think that it might work out.' Her head was bowed a little now. She went on.

'Ray knew a lot of people on both sides of the law, and he sometimes used them to his advantage.' Beth wiped a tear away and looked at me through the dim light. 'He wasn't really what you would call a good man always, but neither was I being 'good' in using him.

'No matter! Ray fell in with the Corson gang and somehow learned the number. Then I think he must have stolen the key. He would have.'

'For you.'

'For me,' Beth agreed reluctantly. 'He was on his way to Flagstaff to open the lockbox and recover Pulver's last confession so that I could convince the authorities to release my brother. When . . . '

'When Corson caught up to him, wanting to get to the incriminating confession first.'

'Exactly. That's when you came into the picture. We knew you had talked to Ray before he died . . . oh, I know this sounds very complicated!'

'Not now that I understand things a little better,' I told her. 'My only question is — what now?'

Really, I saw no way out of this for Beth. What did she want to do, track down Corson and beat the information out of him? The man was a known outlaw with a band of hard men surrounding him. As she had said, the bank wasn't going to allow her to try her key in a hundred boxes, searching at random for Pulver's confession. And, I had no intention of tracking a bunch of hard-cases across the desert, certainly no desire to return to Flagstaff where Tom Driscoll was waiting with my hanging noose on his desk.

'I'll see you back to Yuma,' I said as full dark settled and the stars began to blink on. The coming moon illuminated the western horizon dimly. By its meager light I could see that Beth continued to cry — soundlessly, pitiably. 'I can't do anything else to try to help you that makes sense.'

'We have to continue on to Flagstaff!' Beth said with sharp abruptness, and she rose from the sand, dusting herself off. I didn't laugh out loud, though the temptation was there.

'There's nothing to be done there, Beth. You said so yourself.'

'We don't know that! Maybe the bank will relent if we explain things.' She began to pace the ground with short frustrated steps. 'Maybe someone — whoever the confession was dictated to . . . a friend of Pulver's — knows the number of the safe deposit box. We could ask around! Maybe the banker himself knows the number and would be willing to give it up in the pursuit of justice.'

Those were a lot of 'maybes'.

I was thinking: *Maybe* I could hit the Colorado River by morning and ferry across into California. I was no one's guardian angel. Not at the cost of my own neck and I told her so. She turned, hands on hips and glared down at me.

'Why can't you understand matters! You'll never be free — not even in California. You'll be a hunted fugitive forever. You claim you are innocent, that this Tom Driscoll framed you. All right! He did that for the same reason he sent my brother, Ben, to prison. To protect Corson and his gang from being charged with these crimes. Haven't you been listening to me at all? If Pulver's confession is found, Tom Driscoll will be implicated. If you are innocent, a fair-minded jury will see it, and you'll be free to have a normal life without fearing each shadow and badge you see!'

I didn't answer her then. I couldn't. Beth was right in some distant, theoretical way. But juries don't always go the way you'd anticipate despite evidence. You'd think she would have known that after having her brother railroaded on false testimony. Me, I live in a different world where the hangman is real and death looms. My idea of survival was more basic, that fleeing to California was a whole lot better than sweating it out in the Flagstaff jail while a group of twelve honest citizens tried to decide my fate.

'You don't want to help me,' Beth said moodily.

'I'm not Ray Hardin,' I responded, and on that unhappy note we made our beds for the night.

★   ★   ★

Don't ask me why I did it. I still have no idea. North of the searing desert, Flagstaff rises in a wave of rolling pine-clad hills. We rode higher and the temperature dropped with each mile. Beth did not ask me, nor did I tell her why I had decided to ride along with her. As I have said, I just do not know.

Did she touch my conscience or my need to be protective of a small woman on a lonesome quest? Was I in pursuit of vengeance or justice?

Maybe it was no more complicated than the sad sight of blue eyes crying in the purple dusk of the desert evening.

At a guess we were up at about 4,000 feet in altitude when we began to see the smoke of home-fires from the town itself. It was late afternoon, the sunlight slanting through the pines. Our horses' hoofs were muffled by the pine-needles. It was dusty and warm still at this time of year, but the shade of the tall trees, the occasional gust of cooling breeze, were heaven after the hell of the salt flats.

I had no idea what we were doing here, no idea of how we were going to go about matters.

Beth, on the other hand, was eager and resolute. I marveled at her loyalty to her brother and wondered if I could ever hope to find anyone so determined to do right by me.

'We'll have to wait until after dark, of

course,' Beth said, leaning forward eagerly as she studied the pretty little town below.

'Of course,' I mumbled, wondering about my own sanity.

'Because if they see you, they'll lock you up, won't they?'

'If they don't just shoot me down.'

She seemed to not hear me. This was a single-minded woman. Despite her small stature, her heart and determination were large and magnificent. Unfortunately her determination seemed destined to lead me to the waiting gallows.

'Let's swing down and rest, Beth,' I suggested as the shadows beneath the pines lengthened and began to pool together.

'All right,' she answered. With a small, innocent frown she told me, 'We shall have to sell Henry's sorrel. It only slows us down. Besides, we may need the money for bribery.'

'I can see that,' I said with only a touch of irony. 'Who is it we might have to bribe?'

'Whoever it is that wrote down Pulver's confession, or arranged for the safety deposit box in the bank. Jefferson Pulver was on his death-bed, was he not? He couldn't have done it without help.' Beth's frowning face became more serious, her eyebrows drawing together as she deeply considered her plan to find the papers exonerating her brother. My frown was deeper.

'I can't go down there with you, Beth,' I said in the near-darkness of the mountain twilight.

'Very well, then!' she snapped.

'You know I am on the run. You can't expect me to march into Flagstaff and walk around until I'm recognized.'

'I told you! Pulver's confession may clear you as well.'

'And may not,' I said, shaking my head doubtfully. 'We don't know for sure what he dictated, even if we could find the letter.'

'So you would send me down there alone?'

'I'm not sending you anywhere. I

brought you to a reasonably safe place across the long desert. If you have to pursue your plan, I wish you luck. I just ask you to remember that Art Corson and Sheriff Driscoll will do anything they can to deter you if they have a hint of what you're up to.'

'They don't know me,' Beth argued.

'It won't take them long to find out who you are once you start snooping around.'

'It's a risk I have to take,' Beth said with the same resoluteness she had shown all the way down the long trail. 'My brother must be released from prison.'

She was facing the sundown sky. I put my hand on her shoulder and turned her toward me. 'You're risking your life!' I said and she laughed soundlessly before putting her forehead against my shoulder.

'Am I not?' she murmured, gripping my arm tightly for a moment. Stepping away she told me, 'John, I am not such a fool that I do not understand the risk

I am taking. It is just that it must be done. I could not live with myself if Ben were left to rot in that horrible prison. How could I face myself each dawn?'

I had no answer for her. I stood there in the deepening shadows of the pines and watched as she turned and walked from me toward her little blue roan.

Then, with a silent oath, I trudged after her and swung aboard my buckskin horse. Flagstaff beckoned with its ranks of distance-shrouded lights.

5

We emerged from the verge of the forest and rode on as the velvet twilight shadows disappeared and the clear black sky gathered clusters of silver stars. Just below the horizon the hazy light of the moon again began to glow. I had ridden the last few miles in silence, following the young woman on the little blue roan. Now I spoke.

'We have to talk about specifics, form a plan. We can't just ride blindly into this.'

'What do you think I have been doing all this time, John Magadan?' Beth said a little wearily. She glanced at me, graced me with a half-smile and waited while the buckskin stepped up beside her pony.

She nodded toward Henry Tyler's sorrel which I still led and remarked, 'I told you that I mean to first sell

Henry's horse and saddle for ready money. Our own horses are in need of feed and water.'

'My horse is too well-known in Flagstaff,' I commented. The big buckskin with that splash of white across his chest would be spotted instantly by any stableman.

'Yes — that will take some thought. You might be able to find a small farmer to hold him for you.' Beth went on, 'With a portion of the money from the sale of the horse, I shall buy you a handgun. I notice you do not have one.'

'I didn't have a choice of weapons when I broke away from the law,' I replied sourly. My disposition was growing blacker as we neared the outskirts of the town. Beth, on the other hand, seemed only optimistic.

'Tell me what you prefer, and I will obtain one.'

'Colt Peacemaker, .44 caliber. There isn't any other handgun worth owning.'

She nodded resolutely, glanced at my hands on the reins and said, 'You are right-handed, are you not? I shall have to buy you a gun-belt and holster as well.'

'Yes.' I took in a deep breath. 'Beth, I see that you have a practical plan. For the immediate contingencies, but how in . . . how are we going to set about finding someone to help us discover the safety-deposit box number without getting me rearrested?'

'I have a plan for that,' she said confidently, and at that time we found ourselves approaching the main street of Flagstaff where Sheriff Tom Driscoll, had he known that I had returned, would be licking his chops at the thought of being finally able to stretch my neck. I passed the lead rope to Henry's sorrel over to Beth and turned Buck into a narrow alleyway, thinking for a moment about poking the big horse with my spurs and getting as far as possible away from Flagstaff and a crazy little woman.

Of course I did not. I had come too far to throw in my cards. Thinking of what Beth had said, I began to ride a wide, slow loop around the outskirts of town, searching for a small landholder who might be in need of ready cash and willing to board my horse.

That turned out to be surprisingly easy. I was walking the buckskin down a narrow lane that cut through a stand of pine trees when I came upon a small man leaning on the top rail of a pole fence, his boot on the lowest rail. I nodded to him and reined up.

'How's it going friend?'

He looked at me morosely. 'Wife's mad at me again.'

'What can you say?' I responded with a laugh. 'Would a few extra dollars make her happy? You could buy her a new dress, maybe. Something like that.'

'What have you in mind?' the little man asked.

'I need a place to have my horse kept for a few days. I've business in town, and I don't like the stable-master.'

'Jenkins?'

'That's right.'

'I don't like him neither,' the man said.

He slipped through the rails and approached me as I swung down. He took Buck's bridle and stroked his neck. His eyes narrowed as he studied me. 'Haven't I seen you before?'

'I don't see how. I just drifted in from Montana.'

'Long ride.'

'Long ride,' I agreed as he continued to study the horse. 'So, you see, he's trail-weary and I won't be needing him for a few days anyway. Business to attend to.' The farmer looked doubtful. 'Of course if you'd rather not . . . '

'What were you thinking of paying?' he asked in a cagey voice.

'The same Jenkins would charge,' I answered.

'You wouldn't mind if I saw some cash money? Sorry, mister, but I don't know you from Adam.'

I fished the much-folded ten-dollar yellow-back bill from my pocket and showed it to him. His eyes brightened a little.

'Seeing as you're a man of substance,'

he said with a smile. He patted the buckskin's neck again. 'Besides, I've got your collateral, don't I?'

'You do indeed, friend.' I gave him a crooked smile. 'I'd not lose my horse over a few dollars.'

The walk to town was uneventful and not unpleasant, though I made sure it was circuitous. I wove my way through the pines with my eyes habitually on my backtrail, listening to the subtle sounds of the forest, alert to any movement among the tree-shadows. This was, after all, the town where my death-warrant had been posted.

Where could I find Beth Tolliver? It didn't take a lot of brilliance to figure that out. A young woman on the desert for three days — where would she go? Someplace where she could have a bath and a meal and sleep in a real bed.

★　★　★

The hotel room door was closed, but not locked and I toed it open with little effort. I hesitated at the threshold, lifted my Winchester waist-high, and called out before I entered.

'Beth!'

'In here. You stay out there!' Her reaction was modest but not fearful. I could smell the steam and soap from beyond the interior door. Some kind of woman-scent drifted past as well. I couldn't remember the last time I had been close to this sort of mysterious feminine intimacy. Years, I suppose, before Susan died . . . you don't want to hear about all of that now, and I can't bring myself to talk about it yet.

I sat on the bed. Smiling, I looked at the bed post and saw the black leather gleam of a new gunbelt with a Colt revolver nestled in the holster. The lady had done good. She had accomplished what she had promised me, it seemed. I stood and strapped the gunbelt on, drawing the revolver a few times before checking the loads, flipping the gate closed and seating myself again, feeling somehow more comfortable than I had in a long while.

'You have to go out!' Beth called to me from the adjacent room. 'My clothes are in there.'

'I am not going out to stand in the hall,' I answered sharply. 'You have now got me in a town where they want to arrest me and hang me, and me without even a horse. I don't care to expose myself to every casual passer-by.'

'Honestly!' she said as if frustrated by my constant complaints. 'Then look around for my clothes and toss them in here.'

I poked around and found her jeans and the white shirt, went to the door, rapped once and tossed them in. My mood was not improving. I was hungry, tired, mad at Beth and at myself for listening to her.

'What's first on our plan?' I asked, listening to the small effortful, somehow homey sounds she made as she dressed in the cramped quarters of the bathroom.

'I'm going to the house where Jefferson Pulver was living on his last days. Someone there must know something about who his visitors were, who could have helped him open a safety-deposit box.'

'Just how do you propose to find it?' I asked. The door to the bathroom opened and Beth emerged followed by a thin waft of soap-scented steam. She had brushed her damp hair back and now finished tucking in the tail of her shirt as she talked to me.

The look I got was somewhat pitying. 'You would never make a detective,' she said.

'I suppose not.'

'When I sold Henry's sorrel I simply asked the men at the stable about Jefferson Pulver. He was quite notorious in these parts as you know.' She shrugged her small shoulders slightly. 'They were quite willing to fill me in on all of the lurid details.'

'I see. So now you're just going to the place where he died and ask questions.'

'Of course. Only a direct approach will work.'

'What am I supposed to do in the meantime?' I asked.

'You'll have to come with me. I can't trust to good luck for my personal safety. Why do you think I bought that revolver for you?'

'You do recall, don't you, that I am a wanted man?'

'What you should have done is disguise yourself, grown a mustache or something.'

'Or a long beard. You see, Beth, I didn't imagine ever returning to Flag-staff. I was only a few hours away from the California line when . . . '

'Everyone's plans can change unexpectedly,' she commented as if I was speaking of inconsequential matters. She was sitting now on the window sill, the night breeze toying with her strawberry-blond hair. Quite pretty she was, and I knew how I had gotten myself dragged into this mess but was still puzzled by my own foolishness.

'You also remember that I don't have a horse now. I refuse to ride double with you.'

'That's all taken care of,' Beth said off-handedly, waving one hand in the air as she rose to pace the room, her face deep in serious thought.

'What do you mean?'

'It's simple. After I sold Henry's sorrel I rented a buggy for us to use. It's parked out back. You can see it from the window.' She added as if it were incidental, 'There's a ledge just below the window. You can drop easily to the ground from there.'

I had a fleeting thought of dropping from the window, walking back to where my buckskin was stabled and starting out again on my own across the desert. But just then Beth stopped her pacing, came to the bed where I was sitting and held out her hands, taking both of mine in them. Her smile was brilliant, her eyes sincere as she said quietly:

'I can't thank you enough, John. You

going to all of this trouble, risking your life for a man you've never met and a woman you hardly know. I think you're the grandest person I've ever met.' Then she kissed me on the cheek, her lips as light as a butterfly when they touched me.

I nodded mutely, rose from the bed, and crossed to the window to study the length of the drop from the ledge below.

Once I was down to the ground I waited in the buggy while Beth exited the hotel and came to meet me in the moon-shadowed night. My mood had changed from anger to acceptance. I was now Beth's hero, and heroes must endure, like it or not.

Beth leaned forward intently across the dashboard of the buggy as I guided the dun horse pulling it. My rifle was propped up between us. The night was a close surround of tall pines, black before the rising moon, and tangled shadows. Beth had taken her directions from the men at the stable who presumably knew the way to the house, and I followed her excited instructions, still feeling uneasy about this late-night quest.

'At the fork in the road. Left past the broken oak tree. Now half a mile on.' Her every exhortation was accompanied by numerous jabbings of her fingers. She could not wait to reach our destination. I frowned in the darkness. Her confidence that the Grail lay ahead of us seemed unfounded to me.

At length, with the silver moon riding high we came upon a small house, a cabin really, set on a low knoll. A single window was lighted by a low-burning lantern. A dog barked once and then was silent. There was a rising breeze and it caused the limbs of the oak tree next to where I had halted to wave with slow, ghostly motion.

'Why did you stop?' Beth asked, her face eager in the moonlight.

'I don't like this,' I answered.

'Like it or not, we've got to go up there. We've come too far to turn back now! I'll do it myself if you want to stay here.'

'No,' I sighed. No, I couldn't let her go on without me. I slapped the reins on the dun horse's flanks and it started forward, following the narrow, winding trail to the house on the hill. I saw no horses tied to the rail, none pastured. My eyes continued to search the shadows, watching for stealthy movement or the quick glint of moonlight on steel. I saw nothing.

Still I did not like it. An uneasy feeling knotted my stomach and a little tingle crept up my spine. I slowed the dun with one hand, keeping my other on the butt of my Colt revolver. We were stopped ten feet from the house now and still I did not move, waiting and watching.

'Well, come on then,' Beth urged. 'Are we just going to sit here?'

I set the brake with my boot and looped the reins around the handle. I slid from the buggy to ground-tether the horse. Still uneasy, I circled to the other side and helped Beth down. I might have been more ill at ease in my life, but I could not remember when. Something, a primitive instinct, perhaps, continued to warn me that this was a dangerous place to be.

Beth stepped lightly up on to the porch and rapped on the door. I was still looking around us when the door opened a crack and a sliver of light fell across the warped stoop.

'Yes?' a stranger's voice said from within. Beth answered:

'I've come a long way to talk to anyone who knew Jefferson Pulver. It's terribly important. May we come in?'

'I don't know,' the man answered cautiously. Then: 'Well, I suppose so, step inside.'

The door swung wide and Beth entered, smiling broadly. I tagged along in her wake. I had taken two steps into the shanty when a hand snaked out and lifted the Colt from my holster and I was shoved roughly into the middle of the room. I should have known.

I was spun around and slammed up against the wall. Beth chirped out a complaint, but they paid no attention to her. One man kneed me solidly and when I doubled up another drove his fist up against the point of my chin. I dropped to the floor and stayed there.

I wasn't out cold, but I was on the borderline of consciousness. I could hear Beth's angry voice. She seemed on the verge of tears. I slowly rolled over and opened my eyes. The tall man standing over me grinned broadly.

'No worse than you did to me when you broke out,' Deputy Frank Larson said.

'Who is this desperado?' a second man asked. I started to rise, failed and scooted against the wall to sit staring at the dimly-lit interior of the cabin, my ears ringing. The other man sat in a leather-strap chair, my pistol across his lap. He had an extremely wide jaw and knobby cheekbones, dark hair and tiny eyes. I had never seen him before, but I guessed that this was Art Corson.

'Art, meet John Magadan. He's the man who escaped the noose once. I guess he's back for a second try.'

'Who are you!' Beth demanded. Her fists were clenched tightly. She had backed up into one corner of the room, feeling cheated and perhaps a little angry with herself for not listening to me.

'This is the deputy sheriff,' I told her. 'Name's Frank Larson. This one,' I nodded, 'is Art Corson.' My eyes were on Art Corson's fancy silk vest. Silver buttons, three of them, ran down the front of it. I still had the fourth in my pocket — the one Ray Hardin had ripped from it as the two men fought, before Corson had murdered Hardin over at Coyote Wells.

'How did you know we would be coming here?' Beth asked. Art Corson laughed out loud.

'Lady, I run this town. Me and Sheriff Tom Driscoll. A stranger comes here and starts asking about people like Jefferson Pulver — word gets to me quicker'n lightning.'

'Where's Tom Driscoll?' I asked.

'Out lookin' for you,' Art Corson answered. 'He'll never believe it when he finds out you doubled back on the trail.'

'Look, Corson,' I said, trying to sound reasonable. 'What have you got against me? I've never gotten in your way. Why not just let us be on our way again? Off to California.'

Corson's smile faded and turned into a deep scowl. He glanced at Beth. 'If it was just you, Magadan, I might consider that. But it's not you I want. I want the key to the savings box, and I want the number. It's the girl I want. Look at this,' he growled and he held out the billfold Ray Hardin had taken. 'It was Jefferson Pulver's — did you know that? Ray Hardin stole it from me. Last time I had this there was a key in it. The key's gone. And I still don't know the box number!'

Corson was becoming infuriated. I had the feeling that there was enough in that dying declaration, wherever it was, to hang both him and Tom Driscoll, perhaps Frank Larson as well. Who knew how many others?

'I don't know anything about all of this,' I said, struggling to my feet under the glare of Corson, the muzzle of Deputy Larson's pistol. 'All I know is that I got a little starry-eyed, foolish enough to bring the girl back to Flagstaff.' Corson glanced at Beth and then looked her over too closely, maybe feeling that there could be a germ of truth in my explanation. I tried to put a pleading expression on to my face as if self-preservation was my only motive here. Corson was silent for a moment and then shook his knobby head.

'The both of you are going to stay here until I get what I need,' he said. 'One way or the other.'

It was one of those situations that offer no safe way out. I was going to have to take a big risk, not only with my life but with Beth's. I had two guns trained on me and I was unarmed myself But I did have my Winchester in the buggy. I had convinced myself that there was no way to talk my way out of this. Therefore I would have to move.

I took one step toward Corson who raised his pistol. I stood with my hands spread apart, held high. 'You win, Corson. I do know where the key is,' I said as calmly as I could. 'I'll give it up in trade for my freedom.'

'John!' Beth said with enough panic in her voice to be convincing.

'Now we have things we can discuss,' Corson said complacently. 'Can we reach agreement on this, Frank? After all, he is your prisoner.' A glance passed between them and I caught it. I don't know if rattlesnakes ever communicate with looks, but if not they could have learned something from these two.

Beth had faded into the shadows in the corner, her eyes wide with amazement at the depths of my perfidy and cowardice. I shrugged at her and spread my hands again.

'What else can I do?' I asked her.

Then I turned, spun, and dove headfirst out the cabin window, sending splintered glass down around me in a cold shower, racing toward the Winchester rifle in the buggy while the guns opened up behind me.

6

A wild shot fired from the doorway of the cabin whipped past me and ricocheted off the metalwork of the buggy's canopy. I threw myself to the ground and half-scampered, half-crawled to the rig. Two more shots whistled past me. One of them caught nothing but air, the second ripped through the buggy's flimsy coachwork. As I snatched my rifle from the buggy yet another shot sounded. This one either frightened or burned the dun pony for it reared up, breaking its ground tether and the animal darted off into the night, shaking its head wildly as the driverless buggy rolled wildly behind.

From one knee I jacked a .44–40 round into the breech of my Winchester and fired. Frank Larson, standing in the doorway was a perfect silhouette before the lanternlight, and I did not miss. He jerked back, flung out his arms and then fell face forward on to the porch.

Briefly Art Corson appeared in the doorway and I fired off a second round. He ducked back behind the door jamb giving out a little yelp. I couldn't tell if I had hit him or not, but it was not a mortal shot, because in another minute he reappeared, his arm around Beth's waist, his pistol held to her head. She wasn't struggling. Her eyes seemed glazed over with fear.

'Throw your rifle away!' Corson shouted at me.

'Like hell!' I answered. That could have no good result. But I could not stop him from propelling Beth off the porch. He backed around the corner of the cabin, his pistol still leveled at me. I was a minute too long trying to decide whether to rush him or not, because I then heard the common but chilling sounds of a horse being ridden rapidly away from the house.

I rushed to that side of the cabin,

hoping against hope that Corson had abandoned his hostage as he made a dash toward freedom. No such luck.

Beth was gone into the night, a prisoner of the killer, Corson.

I stood there for a long while cursing myself, the night, Corson and all of creation. I could tell myself it was not my fault. That it was Beth's single-minded determination that had brought this about. I had sensed danger long before we had arrived and warned her. I could tell myself all of this, but in the end, even knowing better, I had agreed to march blindly into the trap Corson had set for us.

I watched and listened until I could not hear the hoofbeats any longer. Oddly Corson had not started back toward Flagstaff where he had friends, but southward, toward the long Sonoran Desert once again. It could be that it was because he had no way of knowing if I might be lying in wait for him along the road to town. Or, alternately, could Beth have somehow tricked him, told him, perhaps, that she knew where the supposedly missing key was hidden? I just didn't know.

I searched briefly for the runaway dun without success, and then before the mockery of the moon I started walking back toward Flagstaff, a deep, dark despair traveling with me.

I came upon the little farm in the wee hours. There were no lights burning in the house, no one stirring. No dog sounded a warning and so I climbed through the split-rail fence and crossed the grassy yard to the small outbuilding twenty yards from the house. Easing through the creaking door I found Buck standing in the darkness, his eyes bright in the slanting starlight as he warily watched me approach.

'We're leaving,' I whispered, 'and not a sound out of you.'

It was a matter of minutes only to find my horse blanket and saddle, one of my waterbags, slip the horse his bit and lead him out into the silent night. I felt like a thief, which in a way, I was.

I had hired the little man and was now cheating him of his pay. I supposed his wife would lay into him again come morning.

I considered these matters and then thrust the concerns aside. Only Beth's safety mattered at the moment, and I was determined to ride Corson down. I headed back toward the ambush site. When dawn returned I should be able to cut sign. Corson's horse was now carrying double, and if Buck was not yet his old self, he was stepping high, feeling eager beneath me as I rode.

As much as I dreaded the thought of traversing the desert yet again, at least I was now away from Flagstaff. But now I had killed yet another man! This one a deputy sheriff. I was in it deeper than ever. I regretted the day I had encountered Beth Tolliver.

Or so I tried to convince myself. The truth was that she had somehow brought me back to life; the truth was that the little woman with the wide blue eyes was the best thing that happened

104

to me in years. I wanted — needed — to see her safe again and make her happy. I barely touched the buckskin with my spurs, but he seemed to sense there was some sort of urgency in our quest, and his stride lengthened into a ground-devouring canter.

* * *

Noon found me under a blistering white sun following the single set of tracks leading across a broad playa. The salt flats glared into my eyes like a well-polished mirror reflecting light and heat. I couldn't understand where Corson was trying to go. I swung down from time to time to take a drink of water and give Buck a rest. I let him have his own drink out of my Stetson. As urgent as my mission was, I wasn't going to push the big horse beyond endurance. That would leave me afoot again on the broad, empty land.

I knew I was gaining, if ever so slowly, on Corson. The gait of his pony had slowed, and anyway his horse could not match the long strides of Buck. I wondered if Corson had some water with him, at least a canteen. But if he had not known that he would find himself out in this desolate country, he might not have. That meant that he, his horse — and Beth — would already be suffering from deprivation.

I don't know what the temperature was, but I know the number would have had three figures in it. The sun was a burning brand across my back. The pale distances shimmered and danced through veils of heat waves.

Where did he think he was going!

My only thought was that he had knowledge of some sort of secret outlaw camp out here. I wondered more than once if there were Yaqui Indians prowling, but there was no shelter, no water for them either, and it seemed improbable.

I wondered once or twice if he was heading toward Coyote Wells, still thinking that there was water there!

I rode on at a slow gallop. The sun began to cant over toward the Western horizon, but there was no cooling promised yet. The land slowly began to change. I saw now red-rock mesas, not large, but low and angry looking against the white skyline, and now again there was volcanic rock underfoot. Now and then a crooked, sage-clotted canyon would open up to the west and the terrain began to grow more familiar. I began to feel more certain that Corson was heading in the direction of Coyote Wells.

Why?

There was only one plausible explanation I could come up with. I considered that it was possible that Beth had convinced Corson that if the key to the bank's safety-deposit box had been taken by Henry Tyler, that he must have hidden it in his tiny cabin. Why she might have taken that tack was impossible to speculate on. Maybe she thought that the longer the ride, the better chance she would have of somehow making an escape. But when Corson did not find the key, what then?

Maybe, I continued to conjecture as the slow heated miles passed slowly beneath my horse's hoofs, she was hopeful that I could catch up, given enough time. It was even possible, I considered, that her intent was to let him lead me far enough away from Flagstaff so that I might be safely away from the waiting hangman's noose.

But Beth, after all, was a woman, and I could not really guess at the labyrinth of her thoughts.

The sun sank with incredible slowness, now hiding half of its face behind the bulk of a fluted mesa. Twilight would settle quickly to darkness on the desert. I made sure that I had a clear reading of Corson's direction, made sure that I had a landmark I could follow into the near-darkness.

Buck was beginning to show signs of weariness, faltering ever so slightly, and I knew that Corson's pony must be run nearly into the ground by now. He would have to halt soon, and I would be there to greet him before the following dawn could see him on his way again. He would not escape, and if he had harmed Beth in any way, the coming dawn would be the last he would ever witness.

The moon was rising later these nights and approaching Coyote Wells from this direction, it kept its face hidden shyly behind the shadowed bulk of the mesa. When it became obvious that I could not go on without risking injury to the buckskin or possibly riding into an ambush, I began searching for a place to wait out the dark hours.

At the head of the canyon where I now found myself there was a small teacup valley, nearly grassless. Perhaps Buck could find enough graze to sustain him. There was no choice. I made my dry camp in near-darkness, a shoulder of the black mesa towering over me. I could not sleep and did not intend to. I wanted to orient myself again by moonlight and try to pick up the trail left by Corson's horse. In the meanwhile there was nothing to do but sit on my blanket, my Winchester across my lap, listening to the small ruminating sounds my horse made as it nibbled at the scant dry grass.

They came when I least expected it. At the moment the moon had lifted its yawning head above the mesa and begun to illuminate my way.

There were two of them. Yaqui Indians who burst suddenly from the shadows and rushed upon me on silent moccasined feet. I rose out of my near-slumber, my rifle in both hands. The first Indian grabbed the rifle's barrel and we struggled for it. He had nearly wrested it from my grip when I stepped even nearer to him and stomped down hard with my boot heel. The thin deerskin of his moccasin was no protection against that maneuver and he howled with pain, breaking his grip on the rifle.

I wielded the Winchester by the barrel and swung with all of my might against the Yaqui's head, catching him solidly. He fell to the ground silently like a pole-axed steer. I spun to defend myself against the second raiding Indian, but he was gone.

And so was my buckskin horse.

I could hear the Indian yell out in triumph as he raced back up toward the head of the canyon, Buck's hoofbeats fading away. I heard the first Indian rise and I levered a round into the chamber of my Winchester. He heard the unmistakable sound clearly in the night and took to his heels. I lifted the butt of the rifle to my shoulder, aimed, and then lowered it again. Shooting the Yaqui would have accomplished nothing.

They had won the little skirmish. I stood defeated, in the deep shadows cast by the mesa. My inattention had cost me everything. Buck was gone and I was afoot on the desert once again. Could I now catch up with Corson? It seemed unlikely. Beth who had been counting on me to rescue her, who perhaps lay awake in the night, listening to every small sound, hoping that I would soon be arriving, could not know that her bumbling hero would not be coming to her aid.

I breathed a series of small oaths, and by the meager light of the pale moon, started walking down the long canyon. Hoping somehow to catch up with Corson and his small captive.

If they had made camp somewhere ahead of me, I thought I still had a slim chance of catching up. If Corson had decided to ride on through the night, all hope was lost. The narrow path along the canyon floor was rock-strewn. It seemed to be nothing more than a game trail. Certainly not many riders ever passed this way. The scent of sage was heavy in the night air. The moon cast a long crooked shadow before me. The canyon walls shoved big shoulders up against the starry skies.

I was perspiring despite the chill of the night. My boots had a tendency to want to roll away from under me as I followed the rocky trail. I wanted to jog, to break into a run, but I knew I would only tire myself out needlessly — if I didn't fall and break my neck. An hour down the trail I stopped abruptly, lifted my eyes and gripped my rifle more tightly.

I could smell woodsmoke on the night breeze.

I moved on a little more slowly, keeping to the deep shadows as much as possible. Sweat trickled into my eyes, burning them. My shirt was pasted to my chest. Every few yards I paused, trying to locate the source of the woodsmoke. There was no tell-tale wink of fire to be seen across the dark landscape, but the campfire might have been doused hours ago, leaving only its signature on the wind.

I had gone another hundred yards down the broken trail before I heard it. A horse nickered in the night and I held stock-still, my eyes searching the darkness desperately. The sound had not been far away, had carried in the still of the night as if the horse were only feet from me. I crouched down, listening for other sounds: a human voice, the shuffling of boot leather over the ground.

Then someone did speak, not in a whisper but in a deep-throated grumbling tone and I found myself shivering with eagerness. Beth was there, just ahead of me. I had to reach her. I crept on, measuring each step, not wanting a twig to break underfoot, a stone to roll beneath my boots. I had been holding my breath without realizing it. My hands on the rifle were slick with perspiration. Pressed close to the massive shoulder of the mesa, I rounded a bend in the trail.

And nearly walked into Sheriff Tom Driscoll's camp.

7

There were four of them in the camp. I recognized Driscoll even in the near-darkness by the red vest he always wore, and by his flowing silver mustache. He was standing beside another man who was seated on a boulder fallen from the mesa's walls. Two more men lay rolled up in their blankets, trying to find a comfortable enough position against the cold, rocky ground so that they could sleep.

This then was the posse that had been sent out to find me, capture me and take me back to Flagstaff for a brief stroll up the gallows steps — if they intended to bother with such niceties. Much simpler to take care of their duties out here on the wide desert. Why bother dragging me all the way back to Driscoll's town?

Were they intending to go up the

canyon or down, I wondered? No matter, I couldn't get around the searchers either way.

Where was Beth!

She and Corson must have met the sheriff if they had come down the canyon, but there was no sign of either. Why? Surely Corson would have been happy to reunite with his partner in crime if he feared I was on his trail. Five men against one surely would have appealed to Art Corson more than making a lone run on a weary horse. I was deeply puzzled.

I discounted the notion that Corson had taken another route. I was not that poor at reading trail sign. The only other solution was that Corson had intentionally slipped past the sheriff, perhaps hidden in an unseen nook or feeder canyon, letting Driscoll and his posse pass by, then continued on his way alone.

Why would he do that? I rubbed my perspiration-glossed forehead with the heel of my hand. I knew nothing at all of what was going on around me, what machinations were in play. Beth had been right about one thing.

I would not make a detective.

None of my conjecture mattered at the moment. I had to find a way to get past Tom Driscoll and his posse if I was to survive and have a chance at catching up with Beth and Art Corson.

I remained crouched in the darkness, uncertain as to my next move while the yellow moon rose higher. It was a time for desperate measures, I knew. I had to get past the posse camp and get down the canyon to the flats where Beth remained a prisoner. When Corson discovered that she had no idea of what the box number was, that the key was not where she had pretended it to be, but tucked down inside her blouse, there was no predicting what he might do.

I took my clue from the real desert fighters, the Yaquis.

Looking into the camp now I could see that three of the men including

Driscoll, were asleep, that the single guard they had posted was looking down the canyon from his perch on the boulder and not toward my position. Their horses stood in a small group just toward the mesa. I took a deep breath, reminded myself that there was no other way out of this trap and then rushed into the middle of their camp.

I triggered off a shot from my Winchester and shouted, 'Indians!'

Men rose from their beds in groggy confusion. No one knew who had cried out. No one took the time to count heads. I fired two more shots up the canyon, shooting at nothing.

'How many?' someone yelled.

'Can't tell,' I answered. 'I'll get the horses.'

With all eyes on the maw of the canyon, guns drawn and ready to fight, that's exactly what I did. Rushing toward the startled ponies, I grabbed the first one I came upon by the mane and swung aboard, firing my rifle again. I stuck my spurs to the flanks of my stolen horse and started it racing down the winding trail. The other ponies followed.

Clinging to the unsaddled horse's neck I rode as hard as I ever had. No shots followed me. The posse was still readying itself for an Indian attack which would never come. No one had expected a stranger to be among them; every man had known there was a possibility of an Indian raid. They still had not caught on.

I rode my horse, a stubby gray, wildly down the canyon trail, the other ponies following until suddenly the draw fanned open and I found myself on the desert flats once again. The gray was flecked with sweat; my heart was racing crazily, beating against my ribcage. Allowing the gray to slow, I looked back up the dark canyon. No one followed; no running man no matter how swift could have caught up with me in the night. Still, my shoulders trembled slightly, a small shudder rippling through me.

The other horses began to wander aimlessly, confused and frightened. I left them to roam where they might. Perhaps I had given the Yaquis yet another gift, who knew? I patted the little gray horse's neck and sat there a moment trying to orient myself. I had seen the desert from this side of the mesa too recently, and was able to pick up a few landmarks in the moonlight. I was still convinced that Beth had talked Corson into believing that the key to the safety-deposit box was in old Henry Tyler's cabin. If I was wrong I had failed her again, but it was the only solution that made sense to me.

I started ahead on the gray. Riding its knobby spine I came to appreciate what a great invention the saddle had been.

The gray — whoever's horse he was — showed pluck and stamina and we drifted southward throughout the night as the moon skyed high and then began to tumble toward the far horizon. We were in white sand country once more. At least the devil winds weren't blasting, but water was once again a major concern.

It was a drear and lonely landscape I now rode across. I wondered about Beth. I wondered if the posse could have caught their horses up by now and resumed their pursuit with renewed determination. Were there more Yaquis around me, hidden in secret places?

The stubby gray horse began to falter noticeably as the night crept toward dawn, and I had caught myself nodding off several times. I wondered if I had the strength for another searing desert day. I both feared the rising sun and prayed for its coming, hoping against hope to cut Corson's sign once again.

★   ★   ★

The dawn was a red promise against a still-star-cluttered sky when I spotted the plodding, halting steps of a horse in the drift sand. I knew the tracks well. I had followed them all the way from Flagstaff. Corson's horse was still struggling forward at what seemed to be a dazed, stumbling pace.

Toward Coyote Wells.

To what end? He and his men had ambushed Ray Hardin there. He must know there was no water to be found. I could not understand this at all. Unless . . . they had ambushed Ray before he had managed to reach the wells. I recalled Ray telling me that. Maybe Corson did not know himself that the wells were dry. Beth would, but why should she offer him any help or guidance? I touched the weary gray lightly with my spurs and he picked up his pace slightly. He didn't have much left in him, but surely more than Corson's staggering animal had. And that was enough.

Dawn rose colorfully across the eastern skies, dull scarlet and brilliant gold. The long flats were flooded with pinks and deep purple where the dunes had been wind-gathered. Within an hour it was hot as Hades.

I found the dead pony a mile on.

Corson had ridden it into the ground, and it lay on its side with blow-sand drifting over it, its eye wide and dusty, with perhaps a question of why it had been so mistreated lingering there. I swung down heavily and went to the dead animal. Its saddle remained strapped to its body and I needed one.

Struggling, I managed to remove the saddle from the heavy animal. After saddling the gray and fitting a bridle, I searched the area carefully. Even in the soft white sand I found the two sets of imprints. A man's large boots and a parallel set of much smaller footprints.

I was no more than half a mile from Coyote Wells. I spurred the balky gray horse forward, an ominous foreboding riding with me. The dawn light was harsh in my eyes, half-blinding me, but topping a sand dune, I still was able to see what I had feared. A bundle, like discarded old clothes tossed to one side of the trail. I couldn't catch my breath; tears flooded my eyes. I recognized the clothing.

Not a second time!

I swung down from the gray before it had come to a halt and rushed, stumbling, to where Beth lay. I lifted her head and then sat beside her, placing it on my lap and ever so slowly she seemed aware of my nearness and opened her eyes. Her smile was vague, distant as she recognized me.

'Corson said I was too much trouble,' she murmured.

'Well, you can be,' I answered with relief and her smile improved. Beth was alive, and that was all that mattered.

'Water?' she asked and I shook my head much as I had when I had come upon a dying Ray Hardin. Except Beth would not die. I would not allow it!

'We have to go on to Henry Tyler's farm.'

Beth gripped my wrist with feverish despair. 'That's where I sent Corson! He may be waiting for you.'

'Then,' I said grimly, 'I will have to kill him.' Not for my sake, not for the sake of the contents of the safety-deposit box, but for what the animal had done to Beth. Had tried to do, leaving a young woman alone on the desert. 'I have a horse,' I said, 'let's get you to your feet.'

'I feel so weak,' she said wearily, but together we managed to get her to her feet and eventually on to the back of the gray which was growing increasingly recalcitrant, with good cause. I started the horse forward, toward the Tyler place.

'Where's Buck?' Beth asked as she looped her arms around me and leaned her head against my back.

'Desert got him,' I said.

As it might still get us. For awhile I was able to follow Art Corson's footprints, and then the trail reached the rocky flats I knew too well, and I lost them. I slowed our progress knowing that the horse was over-used, knowing that Corson, if he suspected I was following him, would be wary and might set up an ambush.

It could be that Corson could not go on and even now lay out on the desert, a dead man himself. It could have been that he was uncertain of his direction — nevertheless we reached Henry Tyler's dry farm without a sign of him. I approached the cabin carefully, from the side of the dilapidated building, swung down and eased to the door, kicked it in, and found the house empty.

I assisted Beth into the hovel and lay her on the cot where I myself had rested not so long ago. I propped her head up and gave her sips of water from Henry's kitchen stores much as he had done for me. I went out into the harsh blue-white glare of the day, rifle in hand, and after a careful search of the yard, led the gray horse to the lean-to stable where I unsaddled it, slipped its bit and gave it hay and water.

Where was Corson? He was not the type to give up. It was most likely that he had simply had to rest. Where? In the meager shade of the brush around Coyote Wells as I had? I was not going to go back there. The very thought of the place conjured up images of death and despair. My idea was to let Beth rest and revive, and later, after nightfall, ride with the rising moon back toward Yuma.

And then?

I could do no more for Beth. I had given it my best shot and failed. At least she would be no worse off than she was before. She would be nearer to her brother, and maybe — with luck — she could come up with another plan to save him. I rubbed the gray down and left him to his hay. Crossing toward the cabin, I still saw nothing, heard no approaching horses, but I was uncomfortable. Sheriff Tom Driscoll's posse might have caught up their horses by now. They could be on my heels. Although they did not know this area as well as I did, if they happened to come upon Corson he could tell them exactly where I had gone.

I was still puzzled by the fact that Corson had, apparently, detoured around his friends instead of joining up with them, but with so much else to concern me, I shrugged that aside mentally. I stood on the dilapidated porch of Henry Tyler's cabin for a long while, my mind tangling itself up with pointless speculation. I was determined to get Beth back to Yuma. But what then? She was steadfast in her mission to prove her brother innocent. If I were hunted down in Arizona Territory, I was destined to be hanged. I removed my hat and wiped my forehead with my cuff. Distantly I could smell the big Colorado River once more.

There was always California.

Shaking my head, I walked back into the cabin where I found Beth on her feet, alert now, looking through Henry's pantry. 'He must have some coffee somewhere,' she said.

'A fire's not a good idea, Beth,' I reminded her.

'No,' she agreed with a sigh, 'I suppose not.'

'Nor is staying here. Corson could catch up. And there's a posse behind us.'

'A posse!' She frowned. 'That must have been who we passed in the canyon. Corson put the horse into a feeder canyon, no more than a notch in the mesa, actually. He said that he thought he heard Indians approaching. He told me to be utterly silent. The horsemen passed by within a few feet of us. I heard a few words spoken — they were in English. Was the posse looking for Corson?'

'No, for me. Tom Driscoll is more stubborn than I suspected,' I said grimly. I sat on the cot, tossing my hat beside me.

'What are we to do?' she asked, leaning against the wall, her hands behind her.

'Get you to Yuma,' I answered.

'Oh, no,' she said firmly. 'I shan't start all over again now that we are this close.'

'This close to *what*?' I asked angrily. Her mouth was set with determination and her eyes were wide and clear. I didn't know if I should curse or kiss her. She possessed a magnificent heart, but an impractical mind.

'To freeing Ben!' she said. Her small hands were clenched into determined fists once more. 'That's what all of this has been for. That,' she added, 'and clearing your name, John Magadan.'

I seated myself again, heavily. 'If you're talking about returning to Flagstaff, Beth, the answer is 'no'. Have you forgotten that I killed another man, a deputy sheriff, there? And there is a posse looking for me. They may have already found our tracks. Our horse is not up to such a long ride, especially not carrying double. And, the Yaquis are prowling.' She started to interrupt, but I held up a hand. 'We have no water, no food, little ammunition. And we have no idea yet who to try to talk to to find out what the lock-box number is, if they would even tell us!'

My voice had risen, and I was sorry about it, but the girl was obsessed, obviously not thinking clearly. I was hot, weary, hunted and completely unwilling to go out on to the desert again, equipped as we were, to ride once more to a town where they wanted to snap my neck for me.

'Henry has plenty of water,' Beth said maddeningly. 'I found two extra canteens in his cupboard. The gray horse will be all right so long as we don't run it, and we take turns riding. I do still have the key, you know,' she said, tugging it up from under her blouse to display it to me. 'When we reach Flagstaff again, I shall inquire of some more responsible people — the banker, perhaps — and ask to know who it was that had taken care of Jefferson Pulver's business for him in his last days.'

I stared at her for a long while. Then briefly I bowed my head, cradling it in the palms of my hands. The woman was insane. Perhaps she had a case of heatstroke from the long hours on the desert. My response was going to be terse and sharp, when I felt her sit down beside me and rest her hand on my shoulder. Her head tilted that way and rested there too.

'You are so good, John Magadan, to help me through all of this. After we have exonerated you . . . '

'Quiet!' I hissed and I put my hand over her mouth. Her blue eyes, eager and hopeful a moment before now reflected troubled concern. I put my finger to my lips and then pointed outside. For above the silence of the evening calm, I had heard something. Scuttling feet, a hasty movement.

'Get into the pantry and stay there,' I whispered.

I crept to the window and looked out. From there I glimpsed a stealthy shadow slipping toward the lean-to and I knew we had trouble. The whisper of their feet told me that the intruders were wearing moccasins and not boots. Their direction told me that they wanted the gray horse. I could not allow the Yaquis to have him.

I opened the door as softly as I could and stepped off the porch, into the dusty yard. I saw three Indians, one with his hand on the gray's bridle. It was not a time for negotiations. I shouldered the Winchester and shot the man through his shoulder, seeing his head turn as he was hit, pained surprise on his dark face. A second Yaqui rose up from beyond the lean-to and fired a large-bore rifle in my direction. It was a wild shot, hastily aimed. My reply was a .44–40 bullet from my needle gun that sang as if it had hit metal and whined away into the distances. He took to his heels, leaving his damaged rifle behind.

The third man rushed toward me, an axe in his hands, thought better of it and retreated. I fired a hasty following shot that caught him in the thigh. His cry of pain was loud and shrill. Not knowing if he would return I plunged ahead into the cottonwoods and willow brush that bordered Henry Tyler's place, more than ready to fire again.

I didn't have to. I saw a few droplets of blood along the dry-creek bottom. I followed them for a way, but the Yaqui had made his escape. Perspiring heavily, panting from the heat and the exertion, I made my way rapidly back toward the cabin, not knowing if other Indians might have been lurking, perhaps even bursting upon Beth in the cabin.

A hundred feet along I found Buck.

The big horse eyed me with reproach as I untied him from the thorny mesquite bush he had been tethered to and led him back into the Tyler's yard. Beth — I swear — stood on the porch with her arms folded as I reached her.

'That's taken care of then,' she said. 'You've found old Buck. Now we have the two horses we shall need to get us back to Flagstaff.'

8

There are times in a man's life when he thinks he has made peace with his youthful recklessness and determines that his foolhardy days have passed. Then some strange passion comes over him and he charges off blindly into folly once again. In my experience, this occurrence usually involves a woman. That is — Beth and I rode northward, widely skirting Coyote Wells, and set our course for Flagstaff.

'What was the name of the judge who sentenced you?' Beth asked. We had been riding in relatively companionable silence for some hours, she on the weary gray, me astride Buck. Our pace was slow; we could not afford to push the ponies harder, although I had fears of swifter, better-rested horses catching up with us from behind.

'His name was Nathan Mitchell,' I

responded at length.

'I thought so,' she nodded, 'that's the man that sentenced Ben to prison. I saw it on the legal papers.'

'And so? It stands to reason that the same judge presided at both trials.'

'Don't you see? We have to know who to deliver the contents of the strongbox to once we open it? No judge would like the idea of finding out he was tricked by men giving false testimony.'

'Unless he is in on it,' I commented.

'In on it? Why would the judge be? I can see Sheriff Driscoll and the Corson gang framing men to cover their own misdeeds, but why would Judge Mitchell go along with such shenanigans?'

I shook my head, rubbed the tips my thumb and forefinger together and asked, 'Why do you think?'

'I hadn't thought of bribery,' she said in the way only a truly honest person could. 'Then who do we deliver the papers to?' she asked, looking up at me from the shade of her hat brim.

'The papers we don't have? Recovered

from an unknown safety-deposit box?' I replied and she turned her eyes away.

'You think I am a little crazy, John, don't you?'

'Yes.'

We continued to ride on silently, though not as companionably as before. The country we were now passing through was all too familiar. Low dry hills studded with nopal cactus and yucca. The trail littered with red volcanic stone. Far to the north, like a shadow more than a landform I could see where the hills began to gather and push skyward. Nearer we would be able to see the pine trees growing as the land rose toward Flagstaff.

The saddle was uncomfortable. The glare of the sun a torture. The horses were obviously laboring now, and when I spotted a jumbled stack of boulders tall as a house, I suggested that we halt on their shady side and take a breather.

Beth only nodded her agreement. I didn't know if the heat was taking its toll on her or if she had decided not to talk to me out of pique. I did regret a few of my recent statements, but I had meant them and it does no good in such discussions to hold back. I would just have to learn to be more diplomatic, I supposed.

I helped Beth down from the gray, loosened the cinches on both animals and gave them a drink of water from my hat. Then I walked to where Beth had sagged into the shade of the boulders and sat beside her, hat perched on my knee. The earth beneath us was warm, but with the occasionally gusting wind and the shade the afternoon was not intolerable. If we waited until near sundown before starting on, the day would cool and the horses would be rested. All in all, we were in good shape.

Except that the noose was still waiting for me in Flagstaff, and the posse was still behind us, trying to ride us down.

And we had no food, little water, small chance at discovering what Beth hoped to find in the mysterious safety-deposit box to free her brother from Yuma Prison. Otherwise, things were going well. She looked small now, and abandoned. I wanted to put a comforting arm around her shoulders, but I did not know if it would be welcome in her current mood. And, I could think of no reassuring words to murmur.

'Have you any money?' I asked her after a while. She gave me an odd look, and I went on, 'I'm trying to think ahead. The horses have to be taken care of. Well, Buck does. The gray we should cut loose near the town line. He is stolen, after all. We have to have food ourselves. I'm nearly out of ammunition.'

'Everything I got from selling Henry's sorrel is gone. We may even owe the stable for losing their horse and buggy! The dun probably made its way home, but it wouldn't do to have us arrested on something as small as that, would it, after all of this?' She laughed a little wildly. I sensed that she was on the verge of tears. Mostly due to my crudeness. It must have seemed to her that I was cruelly indifferent to her brother's fate.

'Let me do the worrying,' I said as softly as I could. 'You continue with the planning — you're better at that than I am.'

I caught myself yawning. I was more tired than I wanted to admit to Beth. The thing was, I had tried my best to help her, but I wasn't providing much help at all. Riding in circles, fighting a battle with the desert ghosts, leaving her in the same position she had been in when I first met her.

I did have one thought.

'I remembered — I do have some money. Enough to see to Buck, enough to find you a place to sleep and buy you a meal.' I fished in my watch pocket and there it remained — the much-folded yellow-back ten-dollar bill that I had taken from Ray Hardin's wallet. I smoothed it out on my knee and showed it to Beth.

'Ten dollars will move the program along a little, anyway.'

She didn't answer me. She just stared, those blue eyes open wider than ever. Her finger tapped the bill on my knee in repetitive fashion, like a telegrapher sending an important yet incomprehensible message. She lifted her eyes to mine, stuttered and gasped and put her hand to her breast.

'Are you all right, Beth?'

She still couldn't catch her breath. Finally she murmured, 'You had this all along?'

'Yes. I took it from Ray's wallet in Henry Tyler's cabin. I never even unfolded it. I don't see . . . '

'You don't see!' Beth said, laughing with humor, with relief or derision or a combination of these.

I lifted the ten-dollar bill and studied it more closely. 'I'll be . . . ' I breathed.

The bill had the two '3s' in its serial number circled in red ink and in one corner of the bill in the same ink was a tiny sketch of something square, a keyhole roughly drawn on its face.

I breathed a small curse. I could not believe I had been so stupid. Ray Hardin had managed to complete his work for Beth Tolliver. When Ray knew that he was likely to die on the long desert, he had thought of a way to convey his information to her. On the face of the ten-dollar bill I had never more than glanced at.

'Box number thirty-three,' Beth said breathlessly, and her hand went involuntarily to the brass key she wore around her neck on that slender silver chain. 'Now we have all we need!'

'Slow down, Beth. Now we still have nothing. Except a hanging town in front of us, a posse behind us . . .'

'I shall march into that bank the first thing in the morning, open the lockbox, remove the papers and have the proof that you and Ben are both innocent of the charges they convicted you of.'

'There's no stopping you, is there?' I asked quietly.

'What do you mean? Of course not, John. I will find this Judge Nathan Mitchell and explain everything. Then Ben will be released from prison and you will be pardoned — why are you glowering like that?'

'We've already discussed it. We don't know what hand Judge Mitchell has played in this game. If he's one of them, I'll be back in jail in Flagstaff, Ben will still be in the Yuma Prison, and Corson and Sheriff Driscoll will be laughing their heads off.'

'That's possible, I suppose,' Beth said from out of the shadows. 'But we shall have to risk it.'

'You think so? Listen, Beth . . . '

'Then, of course,' she said, tapping my knee once again in a different sort of way, 'you will have to marry me. We have spent too many nights alone together. It just would not look right.' She shook her head definitely. 'Ben would not approve.'

I didn't answer; I couldn't. She was surely suffering from heatstroke.

'We have to be going on,' I said, rising. 'The posse is still behind us somewhere. With any luck we should reach Flagstaff by daybreak tomorrow.'

★　★　★

We reached Flagstaff once again at the hour after dawn. It was a beautiful setting with the sun-slashed stands of pines surrounding the town and gentle hills rolling away, I thought once again, but I was good and tired of the place. Beth, on the other hand, was chipper and bright-eyed despite the trail-weariness she must have been feeling. We halted the horses for a moment along the approach.

'Anyone can tell us where Judge Mitchell lives,' she said eagerly. 'As soon as we have opened the safety-deposit box we can ride directly to his home.'

'If he's there.'

Beth gave me a curious glance.

'He may be out somewhere supervising a hanging,' I suggested.

'Your thoughts are too dark. You'll

cheer up when we have recovered Jefferson Pulver's deathbed confession.'

'If it's still there.'

'I have the only key,' Beth reminded me.

'If Judge Mitchell was in with the gang, he could easily have had the box opened by court order,' I pointed out.

'Aren't you ever cheerful!'

'Frequently. In other times. This all started when I found myself standing in the shadow of the hangman's noose.'

'You're innocent!' Beth said, touching my hand. 'Good always triumphs over evil in the end.'

You cannot argue with logic like that. I followed the optimistic girl down the trail toward Flagstaff. As agreed we turned the little gray horse loose at the edge of town. It seemed to me at that moment that my life was running in circles. From Flagstaff to Coyote Wells to Yuma to Flagstaff. Beth, on the other hand, saw her life, her plans, running in a straight line, toward freeing her brother from prison, exonerating me, if she only continued steadfastly with her strategy.

Maybe she was right, maybe her optimism was well-founded. Much of my faith in the way things worked in this world had been darkened as I found myself arrested for a murder I did not do, convicted and sentenced to be hung. Sometimes these small things can dim your trust in your fellow man.

'Beth, take Buck and go ahead. I still can't be seen on the streets of this town.'

'Oh, no, John! You must go to the bank with me. I'll need your protection.'

'I can't be seen, I tell you.'

'Have you ever even been into that bank? Who would know you there? The sheriff and his men are out of town, are they not? Besides where can you hide out without taking the same risk. No, John, you must come along with me and see this through to its conclusion.'

★ ★ ★

We entered the bank as soon as the door was unlocked. A small man wearing pince-nez glasses watched us suspiciously. There was no one else around. The small man was just now hanging his coat up on a hook. Adjusting his spectacles he eased his way behind the counter, the brass cage of his station casting prison bands on the wall behind him. I held back, glancing out the window unhappily, as Beth approached him.

'I need to get into my safety-deposit box, if you please,' she said clearly.

'Yes, Miss,' the man said, seeming to relax a little. 'Number?'

'Thirty-three,' Beth replied confidently. The banker frowned just a little as if he should have known something about that particular box that he couldn't quite recall. He only nodded and led the way, Beth drawing the key up from her shirt neck. No one had told me not to, so I followed along to a cramped little room with a wooden table in its center. About a hundred boxes were set into two of the flanking walls.

The banker eyed me warily again, watched as Beth found the box and inserted her key as if she had done it a hundred times before. I held my breath for a moment. What if, after all, we had been chasing ghosts? But the box slid smoothly from its compartment and Beth toted it to the table.

'We shall require privacy,' she told the banker who nodded, avoided eye contact with me and went out to assist a farmer who had begun impatiently pacing the room, looking for a teller.

The strong-box was two feet long, six or eight inches in height, twice that in width. Now that the time had come, Beth's hands trembled slightly before she opened the lid. This was it — all or nothing. Freedom for Ben Tolliver, exoneration for me. Or nothing at all but the ramblings of a dying man.

'Open it,' she told me breathlessly. I turned the box and flipped the lid open, pretending that it didn't mean as much to me as it did to her. At first sight my breath caught. I thought Beth was going to faint.

I couldn't tell how much at first glance, but there seemed to be ten, twenty thousand dollars inside, all held together with rubber bands. All denominations, old and new style. Beth and I just stared at each other, frozen by the shock of discovery.

'I think the Jefferson Pulver gang was doing very well,' I said quietly.

'The confession!' Beth urged, breaking the stunned moment.

That, too, was in the strongbox, in a legal-size envelope of heavy manila. Her hands still trembling, Beth removed the envelope, glanced inside at the carefully-written confession, all four pages of it and then whispered. 'We have to go. Now!'

I couldn't have agreed with her more. There was no telling who would enter the bank next. We had gotten what we had come for. We needed to examine it somewhere in private and see if we had indeed found our Grail.

'What about the money?' I asked.

'Leave it for now, don't you think, John?'

I did. We hadn't even an idea where it had come from, and didn't need to be caught walking around with thousands of dollars in stolen money. We waited at the door to the safety-deposit vault while the teller finished his business with the farmer. Beth had been able to regain her equanimity, and as the banker came our way, she managed a smile and told him, 'We are through. Thank you, this will set Mother's mind at ease.'

Still looking vaguely troubled, the small man seemed relieved as he replaced the safety-deposit box. Beth turned the key and still desert-dusty, the two of us left, the banker not unhappy to see us go.

'Where's the confession,' I asked as we went out into the sun-bright day. She patted the bodice of her shirt.

'Let's find a place to look it over. You glanced at it, Beth; what's in it?'

'Dynamite,' she said, looking up at me from beneath the brim of her hat. 'Pure dynamite.'

9

We withdrew a little way from the town to have a look at the recovered papers we had taken from Jefferson Pulver's safety-deposit box. In a grove of pines and scattered oaks we came upon a small pond, glinting silver in the sunlight. Three kids on the opposite bank, equipped with cane poles, waited for nibbles. We could hear an occasional giggle across the water. Buck was staked out in a copse where the grass grew low, but deep green. Beth and I found a flat boulder about the size of small kitchen table and we perched on it.

Beth held the envelope in her hands without opening it for a long time. I watched the tips of the tall trees sway in the breeze, heard the squirrels in the high branches; occasionally a pine cone would fall.

'Don't put it off, Beth,' I said. 'We haven't come all this way for nothing.' She nodded resolutely and slipped the long rambling confession from the envelope. We took turns reading portions of it to each other, skipping the places where Pulver willed such and such a horse to someone, left his furniture to his sister, Kay, and such.

Beth had removed her hat and the sunlight through the pines danced prettily in her hair, highlighting it. 'Here we go,' she announced. '*I, Jefferson Pulver, have come to the decision to make a full confession of my years of crime. Not because I have gotten religion and fear passing into the void, but because the skunks I had trusted have one and all abused my faith in them.*

'*One of them, Art Corson, is the skunk who shot me and put me on my death bed. He wanted to obtain some ill-gotten gains which I have secreted away and when I laughed at him, he shot me like a dog, not like the man* who had taken care of him all these years . . . .' A lot of the page was then filled up with calling the other members of his gang skunks, yellow-livered cowards and worse.

I took over from Beth, scanning the letter for the pertinent entries. I read: '*I don't mind dying so much, but I don't want the rest of them going scot free, not after what they have done to me. Here is the way our racket was worked. We would take what we wanted even if it meant killing. Then we would set up some patsy to accuse of the crime we had done. It didn't even have to be someone we knew. It was better if it was a drifter or someone unknown in these parts.*

'*Sheriff Tom Driscoll and Deputy Larson and others, members of the gang would swear that they had seen the fall guy commit the crime. The sheriff would lock them up and his record ended up looking polished, like he was the smartest, toughest lawman in these parts. Of course I paid him real well, too. We had the law on our side and could get away with just about anything we wished . . . '*

'Ben?' Beth said, taking the letter back and after running through a few more paragraphs about how many skunks there were in the gang, she found, beginning on the third page, a listing of some of the murders and robberies the gang had framed other people for. Her eyes were almost feverish as she scanned the confession. Her lips moved as if in silent prayer. Then her expression changed. To delight. Elation. 'Listen, John!'

'I think it was August seven or eight when we robbed the Overland Stage out of Phoenix and relieved them of their strongbox. We were riding horses carrying the brand of a small horse trader named Ben Tolliver. We made sure the stage driver saw them close up. He even became a witness against Tolliver when Sheriff Driscoll hauled him into court. That was almost too easy.'

Beth put the letter down on her lap. Her eyes were smiling, her mouth frowning. I pushed back a lock of hair from her forehead and said, 'You did it, Beth.' I took the letter again. For despite my attempt at calmness, I had to know. Had Pulver mentioned me in his confession? Had he even remembered my name?

I read on slowly, carefully, not wanting to miss a word now. And suddenly I stumbled across what I had been hoping to find, hoping more than I had let on to Beth. 'My name,' I said, pointing at a few lines in the confession, and Beth took the letter away from me excitedly.

' . . . *So that is how we got Tom Gantry strung up all nice and legal,*' Beth read slowly as if hesitant to approach the next few sentences. '*I also recall the murder of Bert Hacker at his gold camp. The man didn't have anything worth stealing, but Art Corson and Jesse McQueen were pretty liquored up and they shot him just to see him die. That one we hung on a drifting man whose name I remember as Magadan.'*

The rest of the confession contained a lot of raving against the dirty dogs who had turned on him and a list of a dozen or so other men they had framed over the last few years, none of whom we knew. I was reading out loud, but I hardly heard my own words. There was a humming in my ears and my vision was blurred at the corners. There may have been a couple of tears in them, causing this. I don't know.

The letter was signed and dated, witnessed by two women who seemed to be Pulver's nurse and whoever it was that had helped Pulver to write his confession down, for the hand certainly was not a man's.

We did not speak to each other for long minutes. Across the blue pond we could hear the kids whooping with delight as they pulled in a thrashing silver fish.

'What do we do now?' I asked Beth.

'We find Judge Mitchell.'

'We still don't know if he was involved or not,' I reminded her.

'His name doesn't appear anywhere in the confession,' Beth said. 'Besides, he is the only one who can pardon you, see that my brother is released from prison . . . unless you want to ride to Phoenix and talk to the governor.'

'I could never make Phoenix,' I said, rising wearily. 'I suppose you're right. We have to try to see the judge and hope he was not in with the gang.'

The sun sprayed a golden fan through the dark pines as we rode back toward town, Beth up behind me on Buck, her arms wrapped around my waist. Beth had been right once again. As we approached the town we came upon a man standing at the border of his field, hat off, wiping his brow with a red kerchief.

'Let's talk to him,' she said, and I slowed Buck. 'Anyone will be able to tell us where the judge lives.'

I was doubtful, but the farmer did

know. He gave us explicit directions, his stubby finger pointing out each turn and landmark as he spoke. We thanked him kindly and started on our way again. He watched after us for a long time. 'He thinks we want to find the judge to get married,' she said. 'I could tell by his look.'

Whatever the farmer thought, we had soon left him behind. The trail was dry, tiny spurts of dust rising from beneath Buck's hoofs. We found the road we were looking for, a short, humped lane lined on one side with elm trees. Beth squeezed me harder as she looked over my shoulder in eagerness. I, myself, was not so anxious to meet Judge Nathan Mitchell again, and we came upon his white, green-roofed house, I slowed Buck a little, wishing that I was far away. But I was not, and the girl riding behind me continued to prod me on.

We swung down in front of the house where a lazy redbone hound slept in the shade of the awning and walked up on to the porch, me straggling behind

Beth, carrying my Winchester loosely in one hand. She knocked on the door once, twice. It seemed forever that nothing happened. I could hear the insects humming in the garden.

Finally the heavy green door opened a few inches. Beth spoke up brightly, her voice wearing a smile. 'We've come to see Judge Mitchell,' she said. The door opened a few inches farther and I saw a tiny woman with a lined face, her white hair in braids wrapped around her skull. She looked at Beth and then at me. I've no doubt that if I hadn't been there with Beth the door would have been slammed in my face — me a lanky, sun-burned, trail-dusty man carrying a rifle. But Beth's smile, her manner, bought us entry.

'He's in his study,' the old woman said, and she waved vaguely down the hallway, tottering away toward the kitchen where I could smell bacon frying.

Beth started on eagerly, I gripped her arm and whispered, 'Be careful. We

160

don't know who might be in the house.'

She continued to lead the way down a dark hallway toward the room at the end. A pair of sliding doors guarded the entrance to the judge's office. One of these stood open, and I could see rows of leather-bound books on a ceiling-high case, the low glow of a lamp beyond.

We entered the judge's study unannounced and I slid the open door closed behind us.

Mitchell looked up sharply, his expression passing from annoyance to concern in the blink of an eye. The man sitting behind the broad, leather-topped desk was not most people's idea of a hanging judge. Thin, almost sloppily dressed in a blue flannel shirt, his dark hair was parted roughly down the middle and plastered back. His mouth was pursed, his brown eyes small, glittering with puzzlement just now. Then he recognized me.

'Magadan!' I only nodded and he asked me, 'Come to get even, have you?' He eyed the Winchester in my hand, but I saw no fear in his tiny eyes.

'Not in the way you think.'

'You must hear us out,' Beth said, taking over. She neared his desk and withdrew the confession from her bodice. 'This is of the utmost importance to numbers of people.'

'And who are you?' Mitchell asked. Beth told him, but the name meant nothing to him. I was watching the judge closely, wondering if he already knew what was coming, if he maybe had a pistol in one of his desk drawers, if other men would soon be arriving, perhaps notified by the housekeeper.

'I beg you,' Beth said imploringly. 'Read this document. It is extremely important.'

The confession lay on the judge's desk, inches from his fingers as he continued to study me, no doubt speculating on what my plans for him were. Then he gave the slightest of shrugs, fixed on a pair of wire-rimmed glasses, and opened Jefferson Pulver's confession.

I couldn't read his eyes, but his mouth seemed to show resignation which after one page of the document turned to frowning disapproval. There may also have been a hint of anger in his expression.

He read very slowly, carefully. There was a brass-bound clock on the wall and its ticking seemed loud in the stillness of the high-ceilinged room. When the judge was through reading, he began again, this time scribbling a few notes on a sheet of paper beside him. Finally he removed his glasses and placed the confession aside.

'If this is proven to be authentic . . . '

'You've got the signatures of two witnesses there,' I said more sharply than I intended to. I was angry not so much with the judge but at the broken system that had allowed these outrages. 'I assume you know the women?'

'Yes, yes I do,' Mitchell answered. 'Honest souls with nothing to gain by deception.' His eyes had shifted away. Now they returned to meet mine directly. 'You can't believe that I knew about this, Magadan. That I would have had anything to do with it.'

'The thought did occur to me,' I said in a chilly voice.

The judge rested his elbows on his desk and lifted the palms of his hands to his eyes, rubbing them. 'I assure you I have never knowingly allowed a miscarriage of justice. But this . . . it could mean the end of my career as well.'

I tried to dredge up pity for the man, but came up short. Beth spoke up, 'The question now is what can be done about it?' Her words became urgent. 'Magadan has been convicted of murder on false testimony. My brother, Ben, is languishing in Yuma Prison.'

'Your brother? Oh, yes, the confession refreshed my memory. I should have caught your name when you introduced yourself. Ben Tolliver. I remember that case now.'

'What can we do?' Beth pleaded.

'I can vacate the convictions,' Mitchell said. 'The evidence in these cases — and half a dozen others,' he said fingering the confession, 'was obviously contrived.'

'The remnants of the Pulver gang are still running around,' I pointed out. 'If they should come across me, they'll string me up on sight, believing they have a warrant to do so.'

'Yes, that's so,' Judge Mitchell said, his dark eyes now showing sorrow and deep concern. 'I'll have to appoint a new sheriff immediately.' He looked at me and I shook my head firmly.

'Never.'

'I didn't think so. I'll find someone, a trustworthy man and draw up warrants for the arrest of Tom Driscoll, Larson and the others.'

'Don't forget Art Corson!' Beth said, her voice revealing for the first time the depth of the bitterness she harbored against the outlaw who had kidnapped her.

'No,' Mitchell said in a voice that had grown weary. 'I should have known. I should have been able to see through Tom Driscoll's masquerade. I blame myself but a judge has to give weight to the testimony of his law officers!' He was silent then. The clock ticked on. 'Is there anything else I need to know about matters?' he asked finally.

'Quite a bit, actually,' I said, and I told him about the small fortune we had found hidden in box number thirty-three.

The judge rose heavily from behind his desk as if he had been aged by the information we had given him. He took a narrow-brimmed hat from the rack and told us, 'I have to be getting down to the courthouse. I have a lot of paperwork to do. After that we can consider what to do about the stolen money.' He turned as if to pick up the confession from the desk top, but I intercepted him.

'I'll keep this if you don't mind, Judge,' I said, folding the envelope and its contents, stuffing them into the pocket of my jeans.

'Very well,' he said wearily. 'I understand.'

With Judge Mitchell and Beth riding in the judge's surrey behind a high-stepping little roan pony, me trailing on Buck, we rode into Flagstaff, following the main street toward the cluster of government buildings, half-hidden behind a screen of adult elm trees. I caught up with the judge and signaled for him to rein in.

'How long do you think this will take you?' I asked.

'If both of my clerks are in, not more than an hour, maybe an hour and a half. Why?'

'Because, sir, Beth and I are going to do something we haven't done well or often lately — eat!'

'Try the Shadow Mountain Restaurant,' Nathan Mitchell advised. 'They burn a good steak there,' he said as he watched me help Beth down, then snapped the reins and started on toward the courthouse.

The restaurant did burn a good steak. They also baked a good potato overflowing with butter. As well, there was someone in the kitchen who knew how to bake apple pies. Trying to make up at once for days of deprivation, I did justice to the meal. I'm not sure that Beth didn't out-do me, though where she was putting it all, I couldn't guess. Content finally, we leaned back and smiled at each other in a way that meant nothing but everything.

When the judge returned we once again proceeded to the bank. Seeing us escorted by the representative of the law the little teller grew suddenly apprehensive, fearing that he had done something wrong.

Re-entering the small room where the safety-deposit boxes lined the walls, we opened the drawer again. The judge made small noises in his throat, riffled through the money without actually counting it, and made his decision.

'We should leave it right here for the time being. I intend to place notices in the local newspaper and in the Phoenix and Tucson papers. Anyone who has a claim against any part of the money and can prove it, can apply to have it returned. Does that seem fair?'

'It does,' I agreed. 'Although I have the idea, Judge, that half of the people who have a claim to any part of this are no longer alive to pursue it.'

'No,' he answered. 'no, I suppose you're right. I don't know what else to do. The money is the one thing Jefferson Pulver was not very specific about. You would have thought he'd have left a clue.'

'No, I wouldn't,' I told him. 'If Pulver was going to die, he wanted the men who had turned against him to be hung. But, if he had somehow managed to live, he wanted to make sure he had money to live well on. Even a dying man has hope.'

* * *

Exiting the bank into the cool, bright day, Mitchell told us, 'I have appointed a temporary sheriff and advised him to hire half a dozen deputies just in case

Driscoll and Art Corson show up in Flagstaff again. I won't send a posse out on to the desert — they wouldn't sign on if I asked them to do that anyway.'

'I don't see what else you could have done,' I commented.

'There are two other things . . . ' Beth began. Before she could finish, the judge had reached into his shirt pocket and withdrawn two folded sheets of paper. One he handed to me. It was a notice that my warrants had been withdrawn and the charges against me dropped. I didn't have to ask what he had given Beth. Her smile was enough.

'Ben will be freed,' she told me. Then she took my arm and clung to it. 'All thanks to you, John.'

That wasn't quite true, but I felt better about the turn my aimless life had taken than I had in a long, long while. The judge was still speaking:

'This isn't going to happen overnight, Miss Tolliver. The warden at Yuma Prison will have to be very cautious that he is not making a mistake. This

170

afternoon, however, I intend to send a telegraph message to the governor in Phoenix and explain — try to explain — matters. The governor will then wire the warden in Yuma. By the time you can ride back there, your brother should be ready for release.' He looked at me, 'Anything else, Mister Magadan?'

'Yes,' I said, 'which hotel in town offers the softest beds?'

10

Judge Mitchell saw to it that we were provided with a second horse, a piebald mare with a cast in one eye. It was an ugly-looking little pony, but spirited and willing and as it came to know Beth's hand, it minded the reins well and provided her with an easy-striding ride.

We had decided to leave at the hour before sunset after a long, sybaritic day of sleeping and rising only to eat once again at the restaurant. We reached the flats once more as sunset flashed deep violet across the land and sketched a long crimson pennant across the darkening sky. Beth had been silent for miles, and it was troubling. Finally she reined up and I circled back to pause Buck beside her. The last light of the day glinted on the gold band on her third finger. She reached out for my hand and asked quite intently.

'Tell me I didn't trick you.'

'You didn't trick me,' I said, smiling at her through the purple light of the desert dusk.

'I mean when I said we had spent too many nights alone out on the desert and Ben wouldn't approve . . . '

'I know what you mean, Beth. Don't ever give it a thought again.'

She smiled faintly, turning her eyes down with apparent embarrassment and we started on through the cool hours, wishing the yellow moon would rise to show us the trail although we knew the road to Yuma well enough by now.

'At least we know now why Art Corson avoided the posse, the rest of his gang in the canyon,' Beth said.

'Now. At the time it puzzled me. But Corson thought you could show him where the key to the safety-deposit box was hidden, and he knew what was inside the box. He had no intention of sharing the money with the rest of the gang if he could help it.'

'Not much honor among these thieves, was there?'

'There never is,' I answered.

The land grew dark and we were forced once again to wait for the moon to rise. Beth was trying to nap, using her blanket for a pillow. I stood watching the night, determined that no one would come upon us unseen. Looking to the north, toward Flagstaff I saw a black curtain drawn over the face of the desert sky. The stars had vanished behind it.

Frowning I considered it. Then suddenly the sky flared to brilliance. A staghorn-shaped streak of white lightning above the hills gave warning. In another few moments the awful bellow of rolling thunder shattered the stillness of the night. Beth sat up, rubbing her eyes.

'What was that!'

'A thunderstorm moving in.'

'Will it make its way this far on to the flats?'

'I have no idea.' Sometimes these summer storms rose above the mountains, flared with violent lightning and grumbled like a giant stalking beast and then simply retreated from the sky as if not liking the broad expanse of the lonesome desert. When the storms did come in, however, they were frequently the cause of dangerous, destructive flash floods, capable of washing away all in their path.

'Should we continue on our way?' Beth asked. She now stood beside me. Gripping my arm and by another flash of lightning I could see concern.

'Probably.' The moon had not yet risen, but if we continued on slowly, carefully, I thought we would be safe enough. Still concerning me was the posse — and Art Corson. I didn't see how the posse could pick up our trail. If they had seen enough sign to indicate that we had been riding back to Flagstaff; it would have puzzled them greatly. They might have followed, but we were now riding south once again, and no one, no matter how good a scout, was going to pick up our tracks in the darkness.

We started on, walking the horses. There were small sounds beneath their hoofs as we passed, nothing more. But behind us lightning continued to flare and the thunder boomed like a cannonade. The wind began to rise as well, and it was by far a cooler breeze than we had been used to, slapping at our backs, lifting the horses' manes and tails.

I saw the vaguest hint of the rising moon's light beyond the western hills, and knew that soon we would be able to pick up the pace and perhaps reach safety by sunrise. Then it began to rain. A few cold, scattered drops at first, and then with thunder exploding over us, rattling our ear drums, it started to fall Biblically. I lowered my head and pushed Buck on. The night had gone dark again, the moon hidden away behind the roiling storm. The rain continued to fall in silver pitchforks.

I knew where we were now, even in the darkness. Coyote Wells was not far ahead, to the east. If we could find the wells again, we should be able to reach Henry Tyler's farm and hole up until the storm blustered its way past. It was difficult to see the land at all in the darkness, through the mesh of the rain. Only by the occasional flashes of lightning could we correct our blind course. Drenched to the bone now, buffeted by the wind, we couldn't have been much more uncomfortable. I had one consoling thought to cling to — no one would be moving out on the flats, no one could possibly hope to find us in the darkness of the storm-battered night.

No one will ever call me a prophet.

For by sheer chance, they had come upon us. I saw four men whipping their ponies, approaching us at a dead run. It was Sheriff Driscoll's posse, and they were riding down on us hard, guns in their hands. They meant to kill me, of course. What they would do to Beth once they recognized her for a woman, I did not care to speculate upon.

There was no hesitation in their demonic charge as they closed ground on us. I did not know if they had recognized my big buckskin horse in the feeble light or simply decided that anyone riding the desert in these conditions must be a desperate man. I didn't spend much time thinking about it.

I unsheathed my Winchester from its scabbard and aimed through the rain at the lead raider. I recognized Sheriff Tom Driscoll by his flowing silver mustache. I settled my sights on his chest and squeezed off a shot. Driscoll fell from his horse's back to lie against the sodden earth, unmoving. A half dozen poorly-aimed shots sang past Beth and me. Two of the men had only handguns, and all three of the remaining men were tying to shoot from their galloping horses' backs. I had halted Buck and took my time, levering through two shots and then a third.

Buck stood stock-still as he had been trained to do and the third bullet from the muzzle of my needle gun caught another of the posse members. I couldn't tell where I had hit him, but he veered aside in panic.

I didn't wait to watch him flee. I fired again at the closing riders, taking one shot at the one man on my left, switching my sights to the rider on my right. I hit one of them, low on the leg, I thought, missed my second shot. These two, whoever they were, suddenly decided they had no stomach for this kind of fight, and they raced away though the driving rain. I sent a barrage of five bullets after them to accompany them on their way. It would have been a miracle if any of those bullets tagged flesh under these conditions, but that was of no concern. I only wanted to let them know that a second try might leave them as their two friends were — sprawled on the muddy floor of the long desert.

We continued on our way, still wary. I

now carried my Winchester free of the scabbard, across my saddle bow.

Beth and I both recognized it at once and she laughed out loud, pointing. 'Now!' she said with irony.

For Coyote Wells, far from being a dry hole, was filled almost to its banks with run-off from the storm. By morning the cattails would have lifted their unattractive heads and begun to green. The stubbornly resilient willows might even have begun to leaf. Wildlife would begin to creep back to its edge to slake their thirst. The Yaquis would return to fill their waterbags.

There was an irony to it, I thought as we passed the watering hole. If I had not ridden mistakenly to the dry wells, believing that I would find enough water to let me continue on my way to California . . . I glanced at Beth and smiled. There are all sorts of ironies in this world.

★　★　★

By the time we reached Henry Tyler's small cabin, the rain had abated somewhat. Still the night was gloom and thunder, and we were damp and cold. I sent Beth to the house to dry out as best she could and took the two horses to the lean-to. I unsaddled them and slipped their bits. The hay was a little damp, but the animals seemed not to mind. They immediately began nibbling at it with enthusiasm.

I made my way back through the rain, stepped up on to the porch and entered the cabin. My first glance around the room sent a chill through me. Beth lay on the cot, her eyes wide open. There was a large bruise on her forehead.

'Finally caught up with you. Drop that rifle, Magadan!'

I shifted my eyes to see Art Corson seated in the single wooden chair. He had a pistol trained on me. The cabin had been savaged, searched with manic energy. The contents of Henry Tyler's pantry had been strewn around the room. I hesitated a bit too long for Corson's liking. He switched the sights of his pistol toward Beth and told me again: 'Drop the rifle.' I let my weapon clatter to the floor.

Corson's small eyes were feverish. He had been long on the desert and it showed. The knees of his jeans were out. There was a three-day growth of stubble across his lantern jaw and knobby cheekbones.

'Back away from the rifle a way,' he ordered. And I did so. Beth had managed to sit up on the bed. She stared vacantly at Corson. 'I couldn't find the key after all,' he said as if we should feel sorry for him. 'I want it now.'

'It won't do you any good,' Beth began but I gave her a look she understood across the room. If Corson knew that we had already been in the safety-deposit box, we had nothing left to bargain with.

'I'll give it to you, Corson. If you let the woman ride off.'

'No.' He shook his head. 'I don't think so. I think she's riding back to Flagstaff with me — in case you try to catch up. If you do . . . well,' he shrugged.

His eyes returned to Beth and I tried jumping him. It was a wild chance, but I knew he had no idea of letting either of us live after we gave him the key. I slammed my shoulder into him and the chair toppled, sending us sprawling on to the floor. Corson still had his gun in his hand. I clawed at it, but he managed to roll away. From hands and knees I dove toward my rifle, figuring it for my last chance.

The two pistol shots exploded inside the cabin's confines before I could reach the Winchester. He had missed me, but had he shot Beth! I glanced at Corson, but he was not moving. He was propped up in a seated position in the corner of the room, his eyes open and quite vacant. I turned toward the cot where Beth sat and saw the little .40 caliber derringer in her hand, smoke still curling from its twin barrels.

I rose stiffly, deliberately and went to sit beside her. Blue eyes lifted to meet mine. 'I didn't want to do that,' she said in a small, shaky voice. 'I never wanted to shoot anybody.'

The derringer dropped from her hand and thudded against the floor. I put my arm around her narrow shoulders and drew her near.

'No one ever does, Beth, unless they're quite mad. He,' I nodded at Corson, 'was a mad dog. There was no other way.'

'I didn't want to do it,' she said again, closing her eyes. The tears leaked out from between her eyelids and streaked their way down her cheeks. We sat in silence for a long while after that, listening to the sound of the falling rain on the thin planks of the little hut's roof.

★   ★   ★

Two weeks on it seemed we were making little progress. The government

184

was moving as slowly as all governments do in all circumstances. Beth and I had been given a small cottage near the Yuma Prison walls, one of a group of six built for the use of visiting officials and other guests. Beth was growing increasingly frustrated with the slowly moving wheels of bureaucracy. She would pace the floor, staring out at the desert for hours on end and then go out into the tiny yard, continuing her pacing there. She visited Ben Tolliver twice a week — the maximum allowed to prisoners. Sometimes we would take a ride out on to the desert. Beth was eager to go out with me, but just as eager to return to the cottage, as if she might miss something concerning Ben.

'It's torturing him!' she complained to me. 'I told him that we have gained his freedom, but each night he has to go back to his tiny cell. Maybe he doesn't even believe now that we have had his sentence commuted.'

'If he knows you, Beth, he knows that he should have faith in you.'

At the beginning of the following week as the sun was rising to scorch the white desert sands anew, there was a small tap at the door and I opened it to find a man in a blue uniform standing there, an envelope in his hands.

'This was sent to the prison mail room. It's got your name on it.'

'Is it about Ben!' Beth asked, rushing to where I had seated myself at the small wooden table.

'I don't know. Give me a chance to look at it, young lady.' Beth drew another chair up beside me so that she could read the letter at the same time.

It was from Judge Mitchell. He wrote: *'I hope you both are well. Following our plan to try to find the rightful owners of the stolen money, I placed notices in all of the area's major newspapers. As you predicted, Magadan, not all of it can be accounted for.*

'Wells Fargo claimed at least half of the cash, proving their claim by virtue of shipping records. A few other small claimants showed up. Some of these

had compelling evidence that they were rightfully due some of the fortune. Of course there were also a few con artists who came just to see if they might be able to cut themselves in on the money.

'Two weeks on, we have no verifiable outstanding claims. The remainder cannot be turned over to you, of course! After all, you did not exactly find it, more discovered it. The city council voted to place the bulk of the cash into a fund to be used for civic improvements. The fund will not be tapped for six more months, however, as other bona fide claimants may eventually show up.

'In gratitude for your breaking up the Pulver gang, and for recovering the stolen money, the council also voted to give you a reward. I hope the enclosed in some small way recompenses you for your efforts and wrongful conviction.

Nathan Mitchell.'

★　★　★

'There's something else,' Beth said eagerly.

There was indeed, a draft on the Territorial Bank in the amount of $1,500. Beth glanced at it without comment, and stood, placing her chair back at the head of the table.

'It's a good start for us, Beth,' I said as I sat staring at the green bank draft.

'Yes, it's fine,' she said distantly. She was staring out the window of the cottage at the high white walls of the prison. The money meant nothing to her, not just then. Not while Ben was still locked up, suffering deprivation and degradation. I folded the bank draft carefully and placed it in my pocket. Then I sat for a moment, watching her small back, wanting to alleviate her suffering, knowing that there was nothing at all that I could do for her. I rose, went and saddled Buck and rode out by myself, a long way from the prison and Beth's unhappy eyes.

★ ★ ★

On the seventeenth day of our stay there a messenger rapped on the door of the cottage. I was sitting at the table mending a strap of Buck's bridle which was on the verge of coming loose, and so Beth answered the knock. I couldn't hear what the messenger said, but the beaming look on Beth's face told me all I needed to know. Her fingers moved in agitated little motions as she beckoned me.

'They're releasing Ben. Come on, come on!'

When we reached the prison we found a solitary figure standing before the Judas Gate. He was of medium height with light brown hair, with evident prison pallor. In one hand he held a brownpaper-wrapped bundle, his personal belongings, I supposed. Beth gave a little cry, released my hand and rushed to embrace her brother. I noticed that his hand started to rise but never quite touched her. Beth urged me forward.

'This is Ben!' she said and her eyes

were beyond luminous. 'Ben this is my husband, John Magadan, the man who worked so hard to win your release.'

The pale man took my offered hand and shook it lightly. His grip was damp and lifeless, and I wondered if they had broken his spirit behind those high walls. He and Beth started on ahead of me, returning to the cottage. I trailed, letting them have their moment of reunion. That was done then. Beth had won her long battle through sheer perseverance.

I looked to the pale skies where the sheerest of clouds swept past before a twisting wind. It had been cooler lately. The desert no longer seemed so formidable. It was time, I thought, to travel on to California.

11

We purchased a stone house from a man who had had enough of the West and wanted to return to his family in Maryland to finish out his days. The house had forty acres surrounding it. The graze was not quality grass, but it was enough to sustain the thirty or so horses we planned to purchase. The area was called Boulder Oaks and the name was an apt description of the tiny community. Stacks of granite boulders with scattered groves of live oak trees here and there.

The house had three rooms, the front room fairly large, consisting of an open kitchen and living room. Two bedrooms faced each other down a short hallway. The thick stone walls kept out the heat of the day and in the evening we would start a low-burning fire in the large, arched fireplace. There was a sense of security about the house, as solidly built as it was. Beth set to work happily from the first day decorating, starting a flower garden along the front wall of the house. I busied myself with purchasing a few horses and training them.

Ben had begun to get some color back in his face, and working around the place had helped him regain some of the muscle that had wasted away in prison. Yet he did not seem comfortable there, living with his married sister and her husband, and I sensed as time went on that Beth, too, was a little ill at ease with the arrangement. Of course she would never say a word, and neither would I.

Nevertheless we were surprised one bright morning when Ben walked into the house and sat at the table with us, his arms folded. He had been carrying his saddlebags and so he hardly had to tell us: 'I need to be going, Beth. John. I will never be able to thank you enough for what you did, but it's time. I still have my little ranch up near Flagstaff, though my horses will be gone to hell and beyond. I need,' he said simply, 'to be my own man again.'

After a few comments about understanding his wishes, Beth and I rose and followed Ben out into the yard. His roan pony was waiting there, and he swung up easily into the saddle. He started to say something else to Beth, but did not. He simply waved a farewell and turned his horse eastward, riding out of our lives.

I studied Beth closely as she watched her brother drift away, wondering if she were going to shed tears. Instead, when she turned to face me her big blue eyes were sparkling and her smile was full and warm. She slipped her arm around my waist and we went into the house. I closed the door behind us.

We do hope that you have enjoyed reading this large print book.

Did you know that all of our titles are available for purchase?

We publish a wide range of high quality large print books including:
Romances, Mysteries, Classics
General Fiction
Non Fiction and Westerns

Special interest titles available in large print are:
The Little Oxford Dictionary
Music Book, Song Book
Hymn Book, Service Book

Also available from us courtesy of Oxford University Press:
Young Readers' Dictionary
(large print edition)
Young Readers' Thesaurus
(large print edition)

For further information or a free brochure, please contact us at:
Ulverscroft Large Print Books Ltd.,
The Green, Bradgate Road, Anstey,
Leicester, LE7 7FU, England.
Tel: (00 44) **0116 236 4325**
Fax: (00 44) **0116 234 0205**